PETRIE'S COMPLETE IRISH MUSIC

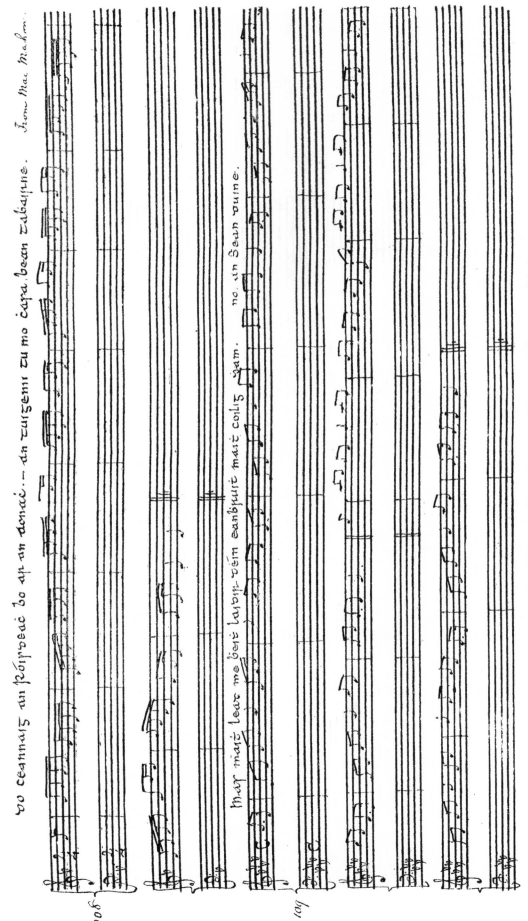

[Facsimile of melodies nos. 108 and 109 (nos. 1498 and 1499 in the present edition), originally found on page 359, Vol. 2, of the Petrie manuscript]

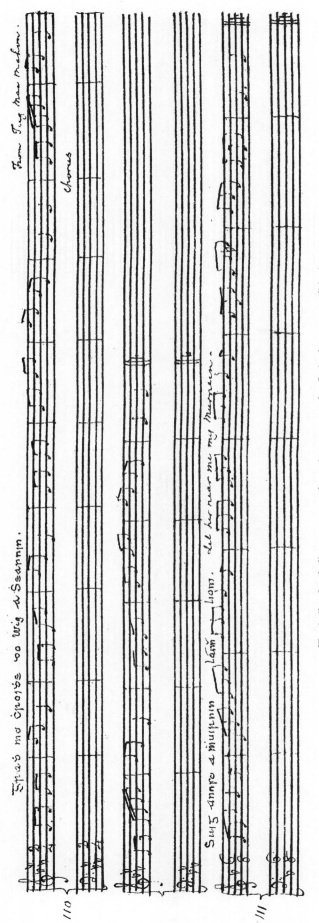

[Facsimile of melodies nos. 110 and 111 (nos. 1500 and 1481 in the present edition), originally found on page 359, Vol. 2, of the Petrie manuscript]

PETRIE'S COMPLETE IRISH MUSIC

1,582 TRADITIONAL MELODIES

Edited by
GEORGE PETRIE

Prepared from the Original Manuscripts by
CHARLES VILLERS STANFORD

DOVER PUBLICATIONS, INC.
Mineola, New York

Bibliographical Note

This Dover edition, first published in 2003, is an unabridged reprint of *The Complete Collection of Irish Music as Noted by George Petrie, LL.D., R.H.A. (1789–1866) / Edited, From the Original Manuscripts, by Charles Villers Stanford,* and originally published in three parts for the Irish Literary Society of London by Boosey & Co., London and New York / Parts I and II copyright 1902 by Boosey & Co., Part III copyright 1905 by Boosey & Co.

The two facsimile turn-pages at the opening of this Dover edition originally appeared as a single fold-out sheet in the Boosey edition, identified as "Facismile of Page 359, Vol. 2 of the Petrie Manuscript."

International Standard Book Number: 0-486-43080-4

Manufactured in the United States of America
Dover Publications, Inc., 31 East 2nd Street, Mineola, N.Y. 11501

PREFACE.

THE publication of the complete collection of Dr. George Petrie's manuscripts of Irish Music at last realises the aspirations of those enthusiastic Irishmen, most of them no more, who founded in December, 1851, the "Society for the Preservation and Publication of the Melodies of Ireland." This Society only succeeded in printing one volume of Dr. Petrie's work. The fact, however (announced in its prospectus), that it had at its disposal the materials of more than five such volumes, set me thinking how they could be traced and if possible published. My investigations happily resulted in the discovery of the material, and it is now presented to the public exactly in the form which it took from Petrie's hand. I am not aware that any collection of the Folk-music of any country exists in such profusion of material or so straight from the mint. A few errors there are, but I have left Petrie's work untouched, only noting doubtful points as they occur. The main bibliographical interest will be found in the collector's own Introduction to the printed volume of 1851, which is reproduced *in extenso*. This volume contained arrangements of the airs for pianoforte, written in a style wholly unsuitable to their character, and the airs themselves evidently (from a comparison with the original MSS.) suffered from manipulation by an ignorant hand. Each melody, however, had a most interesting history and criticism written by Petrie. It was impossible to reproduce these notes in the present collection, but I trust that, at some future day, it may become feasible to reprint them. A reproduction of Dr. Petrie's very beautiful manuscript is prefixed to the first volume. The autograph collection will find a home in the Royal Irish Academy at Dublin.

I have to acknowledge with much gratitude the invaluable help I have received in making this edition from Mr. Claude Aveling; from Mr. Cecil Forsyth (whose admirable Index is a most valuable adjunct to the book); from Miss Drury, who has assisted in the deciphering of the Gaelic titles; and from Mr. James Walshe, who has corrected the proofs of the Irish portion of the Index.

CHARLES V. STANFORD.

October, 1903.

The following are the names of the Council and Officers of the "Society for the Preservation and Publication of the Melodies of Ireland," founded in December, 1851:—

President:

GEORGE PETRIE, LL.D., R.H.A., V.P.R.I.A.

Vice-Presidents:

THE MARQUESS OF KILDARE *(a)*.
FRANCIS WILLIAM BRADY *(b)*.
F. W. BURTON, R.H.A. *(c)*.
ROBERT CALLWELL *(Treasurer)*.
EDWARD CLEMENTS.
EUGENE CURRY.
JOHN C. DEANE.
JOHN T. GILBERT.
REV. CHARLES GRAVES, D.D. *(d)*.
BENJAMIN LEE GUINNESS *(e)*.
THOMAS RICE HENN *(f)*.
HENRY HUDSON, M.D.

ROBERT T. LYONS, M.B. *(Sec.)*.
SAMUEL MACLEAN *(g)*.
JOHN MACDONNELL, M.D.
HON. G. P. O'CALLAGHAN.
JOHN EDWARD PIGOT *(Sec.)*.
WILLIAM STOKES, M.D. *(h)*.
WALTER SWEETMAN.
W. K. SULLIVAN.
JOSEPH HUBAND SMITH.
REV. J. H. TODD, D.D. *(i)*.
W. R. WILDE.

(a) Afterwards Duke of Leinster.
(b) President of the Irish Academy of Music, and a Baronet and K.C., son of the Lord Chancellor of Ireland.
(c) The late Director of the National Gallery.
(d) The late Bishop of Limerick.

(e) Afterwards a Baronet.
(f) The late Recorder of Galway.
(g) A famous Dentist.
(h) The distinguished Physician, father of the late Sir William Stokes.
(i) A distinguished Antiquarian and Bibliographer.

DR. PETRIE'S INTRODUCTION.

THOUGH aware that, in works not of a purely scientific nature and which will be chiefly opened with a view to amusement, a Preface receives but little attention from the majority of readers, yet I cannot refrain from availing myself of the old privilege accorded to Authors and Editors to offer a few prefatory remarks on the occasion of presenting to the public this first volume of a collection of Irish Tunes, which I have edited under the patriotic auspices of the " Society for the Preservation and Publication of the Melodies of Ireland."

In the first place, I feel it due to that Society, and more particularly to some of the most zealous members of its Committee, to state that, but for their solicitation and warm encouragement, it is not at all likely that I should have entered on the compilation of a work requiring, necessarily, not only a great devotion of time and labour, but also an amount of varied talents and powers of research, scarcely to be hoped for in any single individual, and to the possession of which I, at least, could make but little pretension.

A passionate lover of music from my childhood, and of melody especially—that divine essence without which music is but as a soulless body—the indulgence of this passion has been, indeed, one of the great, if not the greatest, sources of happiness of my life. Coupled with a never-fading love for nature and its consequent attendant, an appreciation of the good and beautiful, it has refreshed and re-invigorated my spirits when depressed by the fatigues of mental labour. In the hours of worldly trials, of cares and sorrows, I have felt its power to soothe and console, to restrain from the pursuit of worthless and debasing pleasures, of soul-corrupting worldly ambitions destructive of mental peace, and to give contentment in an humble station.

But though I have been thus for my whole life a devoted lover of music, and more particularly of the melodies of my country—which are, as I conceive, the most beautiful national melodies in the world—neither the study nor the practice of this divine art has ever been with me an absorbing or continuous one, or anything more than the occasional indulgence of a pleasure, during hours of relaxation, from the fatigues of other studies, or the general business of life. It was in this way only that I acquired any little knowledge or skill which I may possess in the practice of the musical art, and, until lately, it was in this way only that I gradually formed the large collection of Irish melodies of which a portion is now submitted to the public. From my very boy-days, whenever I heard an air which in any degree touched my feelings, or which appeared to me to be either an unpublished one, or a better version of an air than what had been already printed, I never neglected to note it down, and my summer ramblings through most parts of Ireland, for objects more immediately connected with my professional pursuits, afforded me opportunities, for a long period almost annually, for increasing the collection which so early in life I had felt a desire, and considered it as a kind of duty to endeavour to form.

In making such collection, however, I never seriously thought of giving even any portion of it to the public in my own name. The desire to preserve what I deemed so worthy of preservation, and so honourable to the character of my country, was my sole object and my sole stimulus in this, to me, exciting and delightful pursuit : and hence I was ever ready to encourage and aid to the utmost of my ability all persons whom, from their professional talents as well as their freedom from other occupations, I deemed better qualified than myself to give such collection to the world.

Thus, as early as 1807 or 1808, I communicated, through my friend the late Richard Wrightson, Esq., M.A., a number of airs to the poet Moore, some of which subsequently appeared, for the first time, in his " Irish Melodies," and shortly afterwards I gave a much larger number to my then young friend the late Francis Holden, Mus. Doc., and which were printed in his collection, and amongst these were many airs, such as " Lough Sheelin," " Arrah, my dear Eveleen," and " Luggela," on which time has stamped her mark of approval, and which have carried the deepest emotions of pleasure to thousands of hearts in almost every part of the globe. For it was from this collection, which—with the exception of Bunting's three volumes— has been the only published collection of our melodies of any importance worthy of a respectful notice, that Moore derived many of those airs which his poetry has consecrated and made familiar to the world. And I may further state that my contributions to Mr. Moore's admirable work, as well directly as indirectly, did not end here, for, subsequently to the publication of Frank Holden's volume, I again supplied the poet, through his Irish publisher, Mr. William Power, with several other airs, which found a place in the later numbers of his " Melodies," and among these was that beautiful one called " Were I a clerk," but now better known as " You remember Ellen."

In thus imparting to others the results of my young enthusiasm for the preservation of our melodies, I never asked, and so never obtained, even the acknowledgment, to which I might have felt myself justly entitled, of having my name coupled with those airs as their preserver ; nor is it from any vain or egotistical feeling that I state such circumstances now, but as simple facts in the history of the preservation of our music that might be looked for hereafter, and which, without such statement, would be looked for in vain.

But to resume : retaining, with even an increasing zeal, my ardour in collecting the melodies of Ireland, I found in the course of a few years that my gatherings had mounted to a number but little short of two hundred as yet unpublished airs, and with a view to their being secured to the public with suitable harmonies, I presented them to a lady, now long deceased, who to other varied accomplishments added a sound professional knowledge of music, and who possessed a true feeling for Irish melody. The lady to whom, with a grateful reminiscence, I thus allude, was the late Mrs. Joseph Hughes, the daughter of Smollet Holden, the most eminent British composer of military music in his time, and the sister of my young friend, Dr. Francis Holden, to whose published collection of Irish melodies I have been, as already stated, so large a contributor. But the untimely death of this most estimable lady prevented the accomplishment of this project after some progress had been made in preparing the work for publication.

Still adding to my collection, however, and indulging in the expectation that an opportunity for giving it publicity would sooner or later occur, I thought such expectation likely to be realised when, at a later period of my life, I formed a close intimacy with the late Mr. Edward Bunting. This intimacy, which had its origin in, at least, one common taste, occurred shortly after the publication of the second volume of that gentleman's collection, and with the double object in view of giving my airs publicity, and, still more, of stimulating him to the preparation of a third volume for publication, I freely offered him the use of the whole of my collection, or such portions of it as he might choose to select. Such offer was, however, accompanied by one condition, namely, that in connection with such tunes as he chose to accept from me, he should make an acknowledgment in his work that I had been their contributor. This condition, however—which I thought a not unreasonable one, but rather suggestive of a course which, in all similar cases, as supplying a sort of evidence of authenticity, should have been followed—had the effect of preventing the accomplishment of my wish that Mr. Bunting should be the medium through which my collection of airs should be given to the public. After the acceptance of some five and twenty or more airs—of which, however, he printed only seventeen—my friend sturdily refused to take even one more, assigning as his reason that, as he should acknowledge the source from which they had been derived, the public would say that the greater and better portion of the work was mine. In my primary object, however—that of stimulating him to the preparation and publication of his third volume—I had the satisfaction of believing that I had been more decidedly successful. The threat, put forward in playful insincerity, but which was taken rather seriously, that if he did not bestir himself in the preparation of his work, I might probably, by the publication of my own collection, anticipate him in the printing of many of his best airs, coupled with Mrs. Bunting's as well as my own continual goadings—and which he was accustomed to say had made his life miserable—had ultimately the desired effect of exciting into activity a temperament which, if it had ever been naturally active, had then, at all events, ceased to be so from the pressure of years, and of a state of health which was far from vigorous. After the devotion of his leisure hours for several years to the collecting together of his materials, and the patient elaboration of his harmonic arrangements of the airs, Mr. Bunting gave to the world the third and last volume of his collections, and I confess that its appearance afforded me a more than ordinary pleasure, not only on account of the many very beautiful melodies which it contained, but also from a feeling that my zeal in urging on their publication had been instrumental, to some extent, in their preservation. For it was Mr. Bunting's boast that, with the exception of those airs which had been drawn from previously published works, the settings of his tunes would be wholly worthless to any other person into whose hand they might ultimately fall, and this I knew to have been not altogether an idle boast, for those settings were—as it would appear intentionally—but jottings down of dots, or heads of notes, without any musical expressions of their value with regard either to key, time, accent, phrase, or section, so that their interpretation would necessarily have been a matter of uncertainty to others, and probably was often so even to himself.

I have thus endeavoured to show, by a statement which I trust will not be deemed wholly without interest or irrelevant to the purpose of the present work, that though I have been during the whole course of my life a zealous collector of Irish melodies, I have been actuated in this pursuit by no other feelings than those of a deep sense of their beauty, a strong conviction of their archæological interest, and a consequent desire to aid in the preservation of remains so honourable to the national character of my country, and so inestimable as a pure source of happiness to all sympathetic minds to whom they might become known. And though, when I had long despaired of finding anyone qualified, according to my ideas, to give to the public in a worthy manner the collection which I had formed, I may have occasionally contemplated the possible production of such a work myself, as a delightful and not over laborious occupation of my declining years; it is most probable that, like my friend Bunting, if the stimulating pressure of friends had not been applied to me I should have gone on to the end absorbed in the completion of works of a different nature, and to which my studies had long been more particularly directed. Such a stimulus was supplied on the formation, in Dublin, of the "Society for the Preservation and Publication of the Melodies of Ireland," and it was strengthened, not only by the honour which that Society conferred on me in electing me their President, but still more by the flattering proposal and expression of their desire to give precedence to my collection in the publications of the Society.

But though this proposal was entirely free from any conditions which I could for a moment hesitate to accept, and though, moreover, I was sincerely anxious to promote the objects of the Society by every means in my power, I confess that I was startled at a proposal so unexpected on my part, and it was not till I had given the matter a very ample consideration that I could bring my mind to agree to it. For, on the one hand, I could not but feel doubtful of my ability to accomplish, without a greater previous preparation, a work of so much national importance in such a manner as might not seriously lower whatever little reputation I had acquired by the production of works of a different nature, and disappoint, moreover, the partial expectations of the Society and those friends that had pressed me to the undertaking; and I also felt that if I did venture on such a work with the desire to accomplish it not unworthily, it would necessarily require for its production the exclusive devotion of many years of a life now drawing towards its close, and the consequent abandonment of the completion of other works on which I had been long engaged, as well as of the practice of that art which is so productive of happiness to its lovers, and so suited to the peaceful habits of declining years. And lastly, as I cannot but confess, I could not suppress a misgiving that, let a work of this nature possess whatever amount of interest or value it may, there no longer existed amongst my countrymen such sufficient amount of a racy feeling of nationality and cultivation of mind—qualities so honourable to the Scottish character—as would secure for it the steady support necessary for its success, and which the Society, as I thought, somewhat too confidently anticipated. In short, I could not but fear that I might be vainly labouring to cultivate mental fruit which, however indigenous to the soil, was yet of too refined and delicate a flavour to be relished or appreciated by a people who had been, from adversities, long accustomed only to the use of food of a coarser and more exciting nature. May this feeling prove an erroneous one! On the other hand, however, I could not but be sensible that, viewed in many ways, the object which the Society had taken in hand was of great importance; that, with an equal hope of success, such an effort might probably never again be made, and that it was a duty at least of every right-minded Irishman who might have it in his power to contribute in any way to its support to allow, if possible, no cold calculations of a selfish prudence, or an unmanly fear of critical censure, to withhold him from joining ardently in such an effort. I considered too, that if, as

Moore perhaps somewhat strongly states, "We have too long neglected the only talent for which our English neighbours ever deigned to allow us any credit," our apparent want of appreciation of the value of that talent was, at least to some extent, an evidence of the justice of such limited praise. I called to mind that, but for the accidentally directed researches of Edward Bunting—a man paternally of an English race—and the sympathetic excitement to follow in his track which his example had given to a few others, the memory of our music would have been but little more than as a departed dream, never to be satisfactorily realized, and that, though much had been done by those persons, yet that Moore's statement still remained substantially true, namely, that "our national music never had been properly collected," or, in other words, that it had never been collected truly and perfectly, as it might and should have been, and that it cannot be so collected now. I could not but feel that what must have been, at no distant time, the inevitable result of the changes in the character of the Irish race which had been long in operation, and which had already almost entirely denationalized its higher classes, had been suddenly effected, as by a lightning flash, by the calamities which, in the year 1846-7, had struck down and well nigh annihilated the Irish remnant of the great Celtic family. Of the old, who had still preserved as household gods the language, the songs, and traditions of their race and their localities, but few survived. Of the middle-aged and energetic whom death had yet spared, and who might for a time, to some extent, have preserved such relics, but few remained that had the power to fly from the plague and panic stricken land, and of the young, who had come into existence, and become orphaned, during those years of desolation, they, for the most part, were reared where no mother's eyes could make them feel the mysteries of human affections—no mother's voice could sooth their youthful sorrows, and implant within the memories of their hearts her songs of tenderness and love,—and where no father's instructions could impart to them the traditions and characteristic peculiarities of feeling that would link them to their remotest ancestors. The green pastoral plains, the fruitful valleys, as well as the wild hill-sides and the dreary bogs, had equally ceased to be animate with human life. "The land of song" was no longer tuneful, or, if a human sound met the traveller's ear. it was only that of the feeble and despairing wail for the dead. This awful, unwonted silence, which, during the famine and subsequent years, almost everywhere prevailed, struck more fearfully upon their imaginations, as many Irish gentlemen informed me, and gave them a deeper feeling of the desolation with which the country had been visited, than any other circumstance which had forced itself upon their attention, and I confess that it was a consideration of the circumstances of which this fact gave so striking an indication, that, more than any other, overpowered all my objections, and influenced me in coming to a determination to accept the proposal of the Irish-Music Society.

In this resolution, however, I was actuated no less by a desire to secure to the public, by publication, the large store of melodies which I had already collected, than by the hope of increasing that store, during the progress of the work, by a more exclusive devotion of mind and time to this object than I had ever previously given to it. I felt assured that it was still possible, by a zealous exertion, to gather from amongst the survivors of the old Celtic race, innumerable melodies that would soon pass away for ever, but that such exertion should be immediate. For, though I had no fear that this first swarm from the parent hive of the great Indo-Germanic race would perish in this their last western asylum, or that they would not again increase, and, as heretofore, continue to supply the empire with their contribution of fiery bravery, lively sensibility, and genius in all the æsthetic arts, yet I felt that the new generations, unlinked as they must be with those of the past, and subjected to influences and examples scarcely known to their fathers, will necessarily have lost very many of those peculiar characteristics which so long had given them a marked individuality, and, more particularly, that among the changes sure to follow, the total extinction of their ancient language would be, inevitably, accompanied by the loss of all that, as yet unsaved, portion of their ancient music which had been identified with it.

To this task I accordingly applied myself zealously, and with all the means at my disposal, feeling that I could not render a better service to my country : and of the success which followed my exertions some correct idea may be formed from the volume now presented to the reader, in which it will be seen that of the airs which it contains, nearly a moiety has been collected within the last two or three years. In truth, that success has gone far beyond any expectations which I might have ventured to indulge, for, aided, as I am happy to confess I have been, not only by my personal friends, but by the voluntary exertions of several young men of talents who have sympathized in my object, I have been enabled, within these years, to obtain not only a great variety of settings of airs already printed, or in my own collection, but to add to that collection more than four hundred melodies previously unpublished, and unknown to me.

Having premised thus far in reference to the motives and feelings which influenced me in undertaking a work of this nature, I feel it necessary to make a few remarks in reference to the objects which I proposed to myself during the progress of its compilation, and which I have kept in view, as far as it was in my power to do so.

Independently, then, of the desire to collect and preserve the hitherto unpublished melodies of Ireland, these objects may, in a general way, be stated as having a common end in view, namely, to fix, as far as practicable, by evidences, the true forms of our melodies, whether already published or not, and to throw all available light upon their past history. By a zealous attention to such points, Mr. Chappell, in his collection of national English airs, has ably, as well as enthusiastically, asserted the claims of his country to the possession of a national music, and, with an equal zeal and ability, Mr. G. Farquhar Graham has illustrated Scottish music in the valuable introductory Dissertation and Notes which he has supplied to Wood's work, "The Songs of Scotland." For the illustration of the national music of Ireland, however, but little of this kind has been hitherto attempted, and that little, I regret to say, is not always of much value or authority. Such as it is, however, it is wholly comprised in the remarks upon a few of the tunes printed in Bunting's first publication. and his remarks upon some fifty of those given in his third and last volume, and even these latter remarks, together with the statement of names and dates authenticative of the airs comprised in that volume, were only made at my suggestion and on my earnest solicitation. But I confess that I found those remarks to be far inferior in copiousness, interest, and value, to what I had hoped for from one who had far greater facilities for gathering the varied knowledge necessary for the illustration of our music than can be obtained now, and whom I knew to have been possessed of all the oldest printed, as well as many MS., settings of a large number of our airs, together with an extensive collection of the Irish songs sung to them, and other materials now difficult, if not impossible, to procure, but of which, strange to say, Mr. Bunting made scarcely any use. To the use of all printed authorities, or such as could be tested by reference, Mr. Bunting, indeed, appears to have had a rooted aversion, and, in all cases, he preferred the statement of facts on his own unsupported authority to every other. Nor would such authority have been without value if we had every reason to believe it trustworthy. But what reliance can we place on the statements of one who, in reference to that strange musical farrago—compounded no doubt of Irish materials—called "the Irish Cry as sung in Ulster," given in his last volume, tells us that it was procured in 1799 "from O'Neill, harper, and from the hired mourners or keeners at Armagh, and from a MS. above 100 years old"?—or who gravely acquaints us that he obtained the well-known tune called "Patrick's Day," in 1792, from "Patrick Quin, harper," as if he could not have gotten as accurate a set of it from any human being in Ireland that could either play, sing, or whistle a tune, and though he knew that the air had been printed—and more correctly too—in Playford's "Dancing Master," more than a century previous. Thus, in like manner, he refers us to dead harpers as his authorities for all those tunes of Carolan, and many others, which he printed, nearly all of which had been already given in Neal's, and other publications of the early part of the last century.

The truth is indeed unquestionable, that not only has our music never as yet been properly studied and analyzed, or its history been carefully and conscientiously investigated, but that our melodies, generally, have never been collected in any other than a careless, desultory, and often unskilful manner. For the most part caught up from the chanting of some one singer, or, as more commonly was the case, from the playing of some one itinerant harper, fiddler, or piper, settings of them have been given to the world as the most perfect that could be obtained, without a thought of the possibility of getting better versions, or of testing their accuracy by the acquisition, for the purpose of comparison, of settings from other singers or performers, or from other localities, and the result has often been most prejudicial to the character of our music.

If indeed we were so simple and inconsiderate as to place any faith in the dogma of the immutability of traditionally preserved melodies, so boldly put forward by Mr. Bunting in the preface to his last work, it would follow that all such labour of research, investigation, and analysis, was wholly unnecessary, and as we are fairly authorized to conclude that he took no such useless labour upon himself, it will, to a great extent, account for the imperfections which may be found in many of his settings of even our finest airs.

This strange dogma of Mr. Bunting's is thus stated: "The words of the popular songs of every country vary according to the several provinces and districts in which they are sung, as for example, to the popular air of *Aileen-a-roon*, we here find as many different sets of words as there are counties in one of our provinces. But the case is totally different with music. A strain of music, once impressed on the popular ear, never varies. It may be made the vehicle of many different sets of words, but they are adapted to *it*, not it to *them*, and it will no more alter its character on their account than a ship will change the number of its masts on account of an alteration in the nature of its lading. For taste in music is so universal, especially among country people, and in a pastoral age, and airs are so easily, indeed in many instances, so intuitively acquired, that when a melody has once been divulged in any district, a criterion is immediately established in almost every ear, and this criterion being the more infallible in proportion as it requires less effort in judging, we have thus, in all directions and at all times, a tribunal of the utmost accuracy and of unequalled impartiality (for it is unconscious of the exercise of its own authority) governing the musical traditions of the people, and preserving the native airs and melodies of every country in their integrity from the earliest periods."—Ancient Music of Ireland—Preface, pp. 1, 2.

The irrationality and untruthfulness of this dogma, as applied to national melody generally, has been well exposed by Mr. G. Farquhar Graham, in his "Introduction" to "Wood's Songs of Scotland," and, as applied to the melodies of Ireland, abundant proofs of its unsoundness will be found in the present and succeeding volumes of this work. I shall only, therefore, state here, as the result of my own experience as a collector of our melodies, that I rarely, if ever, obtained two settings of an *unpublished* air that were strictly the same, though, in some instances, I have gotten as many as fifty notations of the one melody. In many instances, indeed, I have found the differences between one version of an air and another to have been so great, that it was only by a careful analysis of their structure, aided perhaps by a knowledge of their history and the progress of their mutations, that they could be recognised as being essentially the one air. And thus, from a neglect of, or incapacity for, such analysis, Moore, in his Irish Melodies, has given as different airs *Aisling an Oighfear*, or "The young man's dream," and the modern version of it known as "The groves of Blarney," and "Last rose of summer," *Sin sios agus suas lium*, or "Down beside me," and the modern version known as "The Banks of Banna," *Cailin deas donn*, or "The pretty brown-haired girl," and Shield's inaccurate setting of it, noted from the singing of Irish sailors at Wapping. Nor has Bunting himself, from whom more accuracy might have been expected, been able to avoid such oversights, for, in his last volume, he has given us as different airs: 1. The well-known tune called *Bean an fhir ruadh*, or "The red-haired man's wife"—or as he calls it, "O Molly dear"—and a barbarized piper's version of it, which he calls *Calin deas ruadh*, or "The pretty red-haired girl," the first of these settings, as he states, having been obtained from Patrick Quin, harper, in 1800, and the second from Thomas Broadwood, Esq. (of London), in 1815. 2. The very common air called "The rambling boy," and a corrupted version of it, with a fictitious second part, which he calls *Do bi bean uasal*, or "There was a young lady,"—obtained, as he states, from R. Stanton, of Westport, in 1802. And 3. The very popular old tune of *Ta me mo chodhladh*, or "I am asleep," and a modified version of it, which he calls *Maidin bog aoibhin*, or "Soft mild morning," both of which, he tells us, were noted from the playing of Hempson, the harper of Magilligan, the first in 1792, and the second in 1796.

Harpers and other instrumentalists are indeed Bunting's most common authorities for his tunes, whenever he gives any, but I must say that, except in the case of tunes of a purely instrumental character, I have found such authorities usually the least to be trusted, and that it was only from the chanting of vocalists, who combined words with the airs, that settings could be made which would have any stamp of purity and authenticity. For our vocal melodies, even when in the hands of those players whose instruments will permit a true rendering of their peculiar tonalities and features of expression, assume a new and unfixed character, varying with the caprices of each unskilled performer, who, unshackled by any of the restraints imposed upon the singer by the rhythm and metre of the words connected with those airs, thinks only of exhibiting, and gaining applause for, his own powers of invention and execution, by the absurd indulgence of barbarous licenses and conventionalities, destructive not only of their simpler and finer song qualities, but often rendering even their essential features undeterminable with any degree of certainty.

It is, in fact, to this careless or mistaken usage of Mr. Bunting and other collectors of our melodies, of noting them from rude musical interpreters, instead of resorting to the native singers—their proper depositories—that we may ascribe the great inaccuracies—often destructive of their beauty, and always of their true expression—which may be found in the published settings of so many of our airs. For those airs are not, like so many modern melodies, mere *ad libitum* arrangements of a pleasing succession of tones, unshackled by a rigid obedience to metrical laws, they are arrangements of tones, in a general way expressive of the sentiments of the songs for which they were composed, but always strictly coincident with, and subservient to, the laws of rhythm and metre which govern the construction of those songs, and to which they consequently owe their peculiarities of structure. And hence it obviously follows that the entire body of our vocal melodies may be easily divided into, and arranged under, as many classes as there are metrical forms of construction in our native lyrics—but no further, and that any melody that will not naturally fall into some one or other of those classes must be either corrupt or altogether fictitious. Thus, for example, if we take that class of airs in triple time which is the most peculiarly Irish in its structure, namely, that to which I have applied the term "narrative," in the numerous examples given in the present volume, a reference to the words sung to those airs would at once have shown that the bar should be marked at the first crotchet, or dotted quaver, after a start, or introduction, of half a measure, so that the accents throughout the melody would fall on the emphatic words as well as notes; whereas, by a neglect of such reference, even Mr. Bunting, in his settings of such tunes, has very frequently marked the bar a full crotchet, or two quavers sooner—thus falsifying the accents, and marring the true expression of the melody through its entirety, and rendering it incapable of being correctly sung to the original song, or to any other of similar structure that had been, or could be, adapted to it. I should add, moreover, that this rhythmical concordance of the notes of the melody with the words of the song must, to secure a correct notation, be not only attended to in the general structure of the air, but even in the minutest details of its measures. Thus, in Mr. Bunting's setting of the beautiful melody called *Droighneann donn*, or "The brown thorn," given in his first collection,—and which is one of the class here alluded to,—though the tune throughout is correctly barred, yet, from a neglect of such attention, the rhythm is violated, in the third phrase of the second strain, or section, by the substitution of a minim for a crotchet followed by two quavers, and this rhythmical imperfection, trivial as it might be deemed—for the time is still perfect—had the effect of constraining the poet Moore, in his words to this melody, to make the corresponding phrase in each stanza of his song defective of a metrical foot. As thus:—

"For on thy deck—though dark it be,
A female form— . . . . . I see."

In offering these remarks, which have been necessarily somewhat critical, on the errors of preceding collectors of our music—and which I confess I have made with great reluctance as regards the labours of Mr. Bunting, whose zealous exertions for the preservation of our national music should entitle his name to be for ever held in grateful remembrance by his country—I must not allow it to be inferred that I consider myself qualified to give to the public a work in which no such imperfections shall be found. Whatever may be the value of the qualifications necessary for doing so which I possess, the means necessary to ensure such an end have been, to a great extent, wanting. Like my predecessors, I have been, and am, but a desultory collector, dependent upon accident for the tunes which I have picked up, not always, as I would have desired, obtaining such acquisitions from the best sources, but sometimes from pipers, fiddlers, and such other corrupting and uncertain mediums, sometimes from old MS. or printed music books, and often, at second-hand, from voluntary contributors, who had themselves acquired them in a similar manner. And though the airs thus acquired have but rarely borne the stamp of unsullied purity, they have often retained such an approach to beauty as seemed to entitle them to regard, and as would not permit me, willingly, to reject them as worthless.

But I may, perhaps without presumption, claim the merit of an ardent enthusiasm in the prosecution of this undertaking, and of a reasonable share of industry in endeavouring to qualify myself to accomplish it with, at least, some amount of ability. I have availed myself of every opportunity in my power to obtain the purest settings of the airs, by noting them from the native singers, and more particularly from such of them as resided, or had been reared, in the most purely Irish districts, and I have sedulously endeavoured to test their accuracy, and free them from the corruptions incidental to local and individual recollections, by seeking for other settings from various localities and persons: and whenever, as has often happened, I found such different settings exhibit a want of agreement which has made it difficult to decide upon the superior accuracy, and perhaps beauty, of one over others, I have deemed it desirable to preserve such different versions. And as the true rhythm of traditionally preserved airs can often be determined only by a reference to the songs which had been sung to them, or from their strict analogy to airs whose rhythmical structure had been thus determined, I have endeavoured, in all instances, to collect such songs, or even fragments of them, and though these songs or fragments are not often in themselves valuable, and are even sometimes worthless, I have considered them not unworthy of preservation as evidences of, at least, the general accuracy of the settings of the airs, as well as being illustrative, to some extent, of their history, and in all cases I have truly stated the sources and localities from which both tunes and words have been obtained. Finally, I have endeavoured carefully to analyze the peculiarities of rhythm and structure found in the airs, as well as in the songs sung to them, and I have thus, as I conceive, been enabled to lay a solid foundation for a future general classification of our melodies, which must be free from error, and be of great value in illustrating the origin and progress of our music.

That I have been at all times successful in these efforts, or that the settings of the airs now first published, as well as of those intended to follow them, are always the best that could possibly be obtained, is more than I would venture to arrogate, or perhaps than should be expected. My whole pretentions are limited to the accumulation of a greater and more varied mass of materials for the formation of a comprehensive and standard publication of our national music than has previously existed, including, as a necessary contribution towards the accomplishment of such a desideratum, corrected or varied versions of airs already printed, as well as settings of airs previously unnoticed.

The value of these efforts may, however, be fairly estimated from the volume now presented to the public, for, should it meet support, and a few years of life be spared me, to enable the Society to bring the work to completion, this volume will be found to be a fair specimen of the materials of which the others shall consist. For though, by a selection of the finest airs in my possession, it would have been easy to have made this volume one of far higher interest and value, I have abstained from doing so, as the consequent deterioration in the quality of the matter in the succeeding volumes would create a just cause of complaint, and, indeed, I have been so studious in taking these tunes in such relative proportions, as to merit and variety of character, as would afford an average measure of the materials which remained, that I would fain hope, should any difference hereafter be found between them, it will not be unfavourable to the character of the latter.

In like manner, I might have made this volume one of far higher musical pretensions, and probably, popular interest, by intrusting the harmonization of the airs to professional musicians of known ability, many of whom I am proud to rank amongst the number of my friends. But I knew of none, at least within the latter circle, who had devoted any particular study to the peculiarities of structure and tonalities which so often distinguish our melodies from those of modern times, and I consequently feared that harmonies of a learned and elaborate nature, constructed with a view to the exhibition of scientific knowledge, as well as the gratification of conventional tastes, might often appear to me unsuited to the simple character and peculiar expression of the airs, and require me either to adopt what I might not approve, or, by the exercise of a veto, which would have the appearance of assumption, involve me in collisions which I should desire to avoid. From such feeling only, and not from any vain desire to exhibit musical knowledge which I am conscious I do not possess, I determined to arrange the melodies as I best could, to satisfy my own musical perceptions of propriety, and this determination I should have carried out through the present volume, and its successors, but that I soon found that my beloved and devoted eldest daughter, possessing a sympathizing musical feeling, and actuated by an ardent desire to lighten my labours by every means in her power, soon qualified herself by study and practice, not merely to give me an occasional assistance, but, as I may say, to take upon herself—subject of course to my approbation—the arrangements of the far greater portions of the airs which the volume contains. In order, however, to secure our arrangements from grammatical errors, or other glaring defects, I have, in most instances, submitted them to the correction of my friend Dr. Smith, Professor of Music in the University of Dublin, and he has given me the aid of his deep scientific musical knowledge, with a zeal and warmth which entitle him to my most grateful acknowledgments.

Yet—as in matters of taste the judgment is usually more influenced by accidental associations, than by the æsthetic sense of the intrinsic beauty which may be inherent in the objects subjected to it—I am far from indulging the expectation that the general estimate formed of the worth of the airs in the present volume will be at all as high as my own. The young Subaltern will, most probably, consider the last new galop or polka, to which—intoxicated with the charms of his fair partner—he has skipped or cantered round the ball-room, superior in beauty to the finest melodies of Rossini or Mozart. The thoughtless, impulsive Irishman, of a lower social grade, will prefer the airs of " Patrick's Day," or " Garryowen," to all the lively melodies of his country. The popular public singer has it in his power to make an air " the tune of the day," which, however high its merits, might have remained unknown but for his patronage. The people of every different race and country will not be persuaded that there is any national music in the world equal to their own, for it is expressive of their own musical sensations, and is associated with the songs and recollections of their youth. And thus the finest of our Irish melodies have obtained their just appreciation far less from any immediate estimate of their merits, than from their accidental union with the lyrics of Moore and others, which had taken a hold on the popular mind.

The airs presented to the public in this work have no such accidental associations, and no such interpreters of their meanings, to recommend them to general favour : and hence, they will have not only to encounter the prejudices of those who believe that all the Irish melodies worthy of preservation have been already collected—an opinion fostered in the public mind by Moore and Bunting—but the still greater danger of disappointing the expectations of those who believe that airs presented to their ears for the first time, and without words, should at once take possession of their feelings, and give as much delight as those which had been embalmed there by various extrinsic associations.

But, though it is only natural to conclude that, as the best melodies of every country would, at least generally, be the most popular, and, therefore, the first to present themselves to notice, and be appropriated by early collectors, those which remained to reward the industry of subsequent collectors—gleaners on an already reaped field—would be of an inferior quality, yet I cannot but indulge the belief that the airs in this work will, on the whole, be found to possess as great an amount of variety and excellence as belong to those which have preceded it, and that, should the support necessary to its completion be awarded to it, it will afford a valuable and enduring contribution to the store of simple pleasures necessary to minds of a refined and sensitive nature, and greatly add to the respect which Ireland has already obtained from the world from the beauty of her national music.

GEORGE PETRIE.

67, Rathmines Road,
    1st May, 1855.

INDEX.

NOTE.—*The numbers given refer to the tunes and not to the pages.*

I.

TUNES WITHOUT TITLES.

1 to 95, 97 to 100, 102 to 288, 324, 411, 433, 480, 485, 489, 496, 839, 862, 1058, 1059, 1060, 1279, 1281, 1282, 1286, 1329, 1579.

II.

TUNES WITH ENGLISH TITLES.

III.

TUNES WITH IRISH TITLES.

IV.

JIGS AND HOP JIGS.

Jigs.—96, 477, 920 to 977, 981, 982, 984, 1000, 1109, 1120, 1258, 1265. 1535.
Hop Jigs.—978, 979, 980, 1118, 1408.

V.

REELS.

352, 396, 397, 457, 458, 462, 484, 703, 884 to 891, 893 to 918.

VI.

MARCHES.

158, 409, 448, 487, 966, 982 to 1001, 1272, 1312, 1318, 1424, 1425, 1465.

VII.

CAOINES, LAMENTS, HYMNS, ETC.

438, 1018 to 1050, 1097, 1161, 1176, 1202, 1205, 1287, 1315, 1316, 1317, 1470.

VIII.

NURSE SONGS AND LULLABIES.

1002 to 1017.   *See also* 1411, 1412, 1413, 1465.

IX.

PLANXTIES AND DANCES.

101, 499, 504, 588, 786, 870 to 883, 919, 1416, 1450.

X.

PLOUGH WHISTLES.

1051, 1052, 1053, 1054, 1055, 1102.

XI.

SPINNING AND WEAVING TUNES.

1172 to 1175, 1368, 1369, 1473 to 1475, 1545.

XII.

The following is a complete list of those tunes of which the place-sources are expressly indicated by PETRIE :—

America (North).—866.
Armagh Co.—384, 850.
Arran More.—273 to 281, 296, 299, 322, 323, 324, 327, 332, 335, 336, 371, 372, 374 to 379, 816 to 819, 1119, 1137, 1277.
Askeaton.—1233.
Ballyorgan.—914, 932, 1008.
Bannagher.—1038, 1196, 1267, 1268.
Belfast.—863.
Bellaghy.—698.
Bennada Glens.—651, 1029, 1197, 1199, 1200, 1268.
Camber (Parish of).—559.
Carlow.—686, 691.
Cavan.—507, 536, 561, 637, 638, 824, 844.
Clare.—166 to 182, 448, 462, 723, 792, 871, 905 to 908, 940 to 944, 979, 984, 1003, 1173, 1219, 1304, 1318, 1366, 1367, 1404, 1542, 1545.
Clonakilty.—1167.
Connaught.—474 (?), 758, 909, 935 to 939, 995, 1109, 1327, 1328, 1535.
Connemara.—910, 1107, 1549.
Cork.—300, 370, 396, 397, 468, 703, 704, 884, 885, 886, 895, 900 to 904, 918, 945, 946, 947, 1005, 1240, 1290.
Donegal Co.—365, 388, 512, 678, 808, 846, 1047, 1325.
Dublin.—183 to 186, 297, 328, 474 (?), 643, 682, 683, 755, 799, 1412.
Dungiven.—438, 661, 790.
Erris.—383, 1223, 1224.
Galway (including the Claddagh).—304, 417, 421, 445, 645, 822, 951, 1040, 1050, 1437.
Iverk.—618, 853.
Kerry.—308 (?) 736, 738, 899, 956, 1103, 1232, 1405.
Kilfinane.—243, 555, 1141.
Kilkenny.—55, 190, 334, 772, 843, 852.
Kilmallock.—1165.
Kilrush.—283, 473, 611, 1252, 1394 to 1397, 1427.
King's Co.—292, 604.
Leinster.—1032.
Leitrim.—603, 911, 952 to 955.
Limerick (including Glenosheen and Coolfree).—226, 228, 229, 235, 248, 250, 293, 294, 531, 792, 823, 862, 879, 887, 931, 949, 958, 964, 965, 1238, 1407, 1412, 1439, 1562.
Londonderry Co.—289, 302, 303, 325, 337, 407, 674, 757, 840, 841, 1018, 1021, 1043, 1049, 1060, 1061, 1062, 1302, 1320.
Louth.—191, 713, 768, 1201, 1579.
Man (Isle of).—717, 773.
Mayo.—201, 246, 380, 382, 494, 786, 794, 795, 950, 1019, 1105, 1123, 1125, 1126, 1177, 1185, 1198, 1225, 1269, 1568.
Monaghan.—529, 1015.
Munster.—208, 457, 458, 582, 813, 839, 875, 888 to 894, 896, 897, 920 to 925, 927 to 934, 982, 1032, 1116, 1204, 1212, 1217, 1258, 1265, 1295, 1408.
Roscommon.—489, 1020.
Rosmore.—742.
Skull.—389, 390, 1075, 1082.
Slane.—1273.
Slieve Gullan.—1213.
Sligo.—207 to 214, 948, 1004, 1098, 1220, 1221, 1222.
Tipperary.—55.
Tuam.—391, 1180.
Tyrone Co.—345, 644, 747, 772, 820.
Waterford Co.—55, 215, 450, 696.
West Meath.—769.
Westport.—701.
Wexford.—659, 685, 777 to 785, 787.
Wicklow.—859.

NOTE.

THE foregoing tunes are contained in the Petrie manuscript, pp. 1 to 862. Besides these, there are scattered references, throughout the three volumes, to eighteen other pages (863—880). Of these no trace can now be found. They were probably made up principally of harmonized versions of tunes with Gaelic titles.

The total number of tunes contained in the Petrie manuscript is 2148, of which more than 500 are duplicates and slight variants.

In addition to the titles given above, one occurs on p. 741 (" Bring Biddy home,— Galway, 28th August, 1840 ") with a blank space where the tune should be.

ED.

The Petrie Collection of Irish Music.

PART I

+)Airs without titles are so in the original, or are marked "Name unknown" or "anonymous."

2

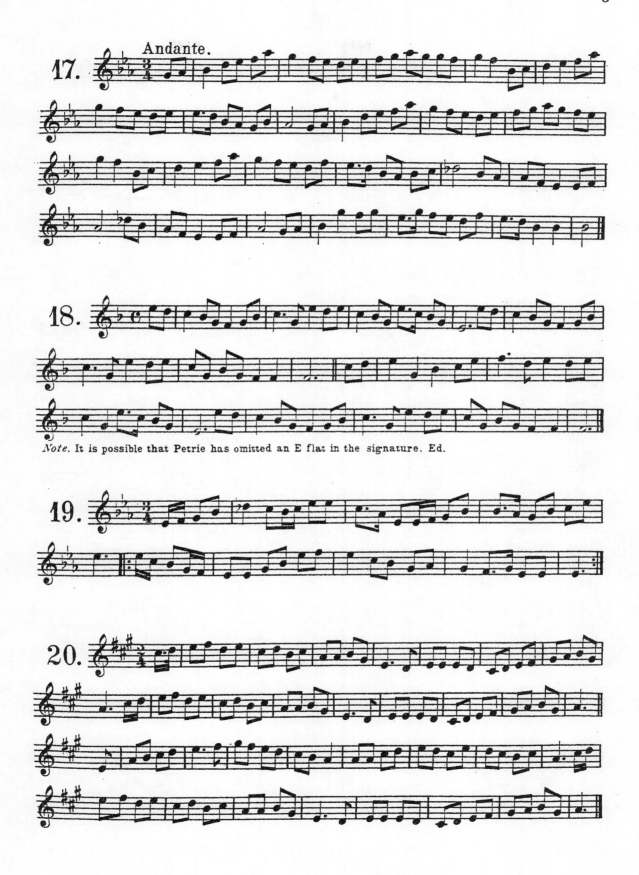

Note. It is possible that Petrie has omitted an E flat in the signature. Ed.

6

Note. Petrie writes "A charming air." The curious A natural is his. Ed.

34.

Note. Variant of Nº 33 Ed.

35.

Note. Variant Nº 33. Ed.

36.

37.

11

46.

47.

48.

Note. A slight variant of Nº 26. Ed.

49.

Note. These sharps are added in pencil. Ed.

Note. Same as preceding, a semitone higher, without the chorus.

14

"One of the most admired airs in the three neighbouring counties of Kilkenny, Tipperary and Waterford"—Petrie.

With Spirit.

Chorus.

Note. This tune appears again in the manuscript, but without the repeat marked at the end of the first phrase. Ed.

16

See Nº 1. of which it is a slight variant. Ed.

From P. Carew's MSS.

Allegretto con spirito.

Second setting of above.

Third setting. (Munster Jig.) Buachalin Bruithe.

From Mr. Joyce.

Allegro moderato.

98.

99.

100.

"Here we go up, up, up." Called "Mad Moll" in the 17th Edition of the Dancing Master. 1721.

101.

106.

107.

Note. A variant of Nº 136. Ed.

108.

28

30

117.

118.

119. Allegretto.   from a Ballad Singer: 25. Aug. 1864.

120.

121. Allegretto.

+ Another Version has F♮ here. Ed.

34

Note. A variant of No 107. Ed.

139.

140.

Note. A variant of N⁰ 72.

141.

142.

Fin.

D. C.

Andantino.

143.

144.

Note. Cf. Nº 183 and 184. Ed.

145.

38

155.

156.

157.

Quick March Time.

158.

39

40

163.

164.

Air. Name unknown.

Set by P. W. Joyce Esq. from
Peggy Cudmore.

165.

C?. Clare.

From F. Keane

166.

42

Co Clare.   Kilrush air.

167.

Co Clare.   From F. Keane.

168.

Co Clare.   From F. Keane.

169.

Co Clare.   From F. Keane.

170.

Cº Clare.

From F. Keane, 10. Sep. 1854.

171.

Cº Clare.

From F. Keane.

172.

Allegretto.

Cº Clare.

From F. Keane.

173.

Note. The small notes shew the variants in another setting, which is otherwise identical. Ed.

Cº Clare.

From F. Keane, 12. July 1858.

174.

Note. A Signature of two sharps has been added in pencil by another hand. Ed.   H. 3279

44

Cº Clare.

from F. Keane.

175.

Note. A variant of Nº 171. Ed.

Cº Clare.

from F. Keane 19. July 1858.

176.

Note. The MS. has Signature and accidentals (♯) added in pencil. Ed.

Cº Clare.

from F. Keane 19. July 1858.

177.

45

Note. A variant of preceding tune ED.

46

181.

Allegretto.

Note. Another setting of No. 176. MS. has signature, and accidentals in pencil, compare also the following tune. Ed.

Co. Clare.

from F. Keane's book.

182.

Andante.

from a Dublin Ballad singer.

183.

from a Ballad singer at Rathmines Dublin.

184.

Variant of preceding.

from a blind man singing in Cuffe Street, Dublin, Nov. 1852.

as sung by a Ballad singer at Rathmines.

from Mr. R. Fitzgerald.

from R. Fitzgerald.

from Mr. R. Fitzgerald.

189.

Kilkenny air.

190.

from the county of Louth.

191.

Name unknown.

from P. Mac Dowell Esq.

192.

from P. MacDowell.

193.

from P. MacDowell Esq.

194. Moderato.

from P. MacDowell Esq. March 1859.

195. Allegretto.

Chorus.

From Mr. MacDowell.

196.

From Mr Mac Dowell.

197.

A variant of N.º 39. Ed.

From Mr Hardiman's M.S.

198.

From Mary Madden.

199.

From Mary Madden. Aug. 1854.

200.

Mayo air. Name unknown.

From Dr. Kelly.

Andante.

201.

202. From T. Mac Mahon.

203. Allegretto. From T. Mc. Mahon. May. 56

204. Name unascertained. Andante. From M.r Pigot's M.S.

205. From E. O' Reilly's M. S.

52

206.   Set at Rathcarrick Cº Sligo.

207.   Set at Rathcarrick CºSligo.

208.   Sligo & Munster.

Note. This air, which is without title in the M S., is published in Petrie's Ancient Music of Ireland, Vol. I. as "The blackthorn cane with a thong."

209.   Sligo air.

Variant of Preceding.

210.   Sligo air.

A Sligo air.

211.

A Sligo air.

212.

A Sligo air.

213.

Peasant air; set at Screen, County of Sligo, by Miss M E Stokes.

214.

54

County of Waterford air.   From Mr. Fitzgerald.

215.

Allegretto.   From Father Walsh.

216.

From Father Walsh.

217.

A Kerry air without name.   From Father Walsh.

218.

From Mr Joyce.

219.

Chorus.

From Mr P. Joyce.

220.

From Patrick Joyce Eq.

221.

Chorus.

Set by Mr Joyce from J. Martin. August 1854.

222.

Set from M. Dineen by Mr Joyce.

223.

From Mr Joyce.

224.

Andante.

From Mr Joyce.

225.

Set by Mr Joyce, From Lewis O'Brien. Coolfree.

Andante.

226.

Andante.

From Mr Joyce.

227.

? Ed.

58

60

242. Andante. From Mr Joyce.

243. Andante. Mr Joyce, from Denis Hayes, Kilfinane.

244. Allegretto. Mr Joyce, from D. Condon.

245. Andante. Mr Joyce, from J. Martin.

From the neighbourhood Long Con, Cᵒ Mayo.

P.W. Joyce.

From Mʳ Joyce.

Allegretto.

Note. A slight variant of Nº 10. Ed.

Set from Mʳˢ Magrath - Glenosheen.

From Mʳ Joyce.

Andante.

This tune appears several times
One version has B♭ corrected to C in pencil at ∗ Ed.

Set from Edward Goggin, by Mʳ Joyce.

Air. From the singing of Mʳˢ Magrath- Glenosheen Co. Limerick.

Mʳ Joyce.

250.

Note. Variant of Nº 248.

251.

Note. Signature omitted in MS. Ed.
This air is published in Petrie's Ancient Music of Ireland, Vol. I. under the title of "When she answered me her voice was low" from Cº Cavan. Ed.

252.

253.

Note. This air is printed by Petrie (in "Ancient Music of Ireland") in the minor. Ed.

64

A variant of Nos 208 and 209. Ed.

A slight variant of Nos 72. and 140. Ed.

66

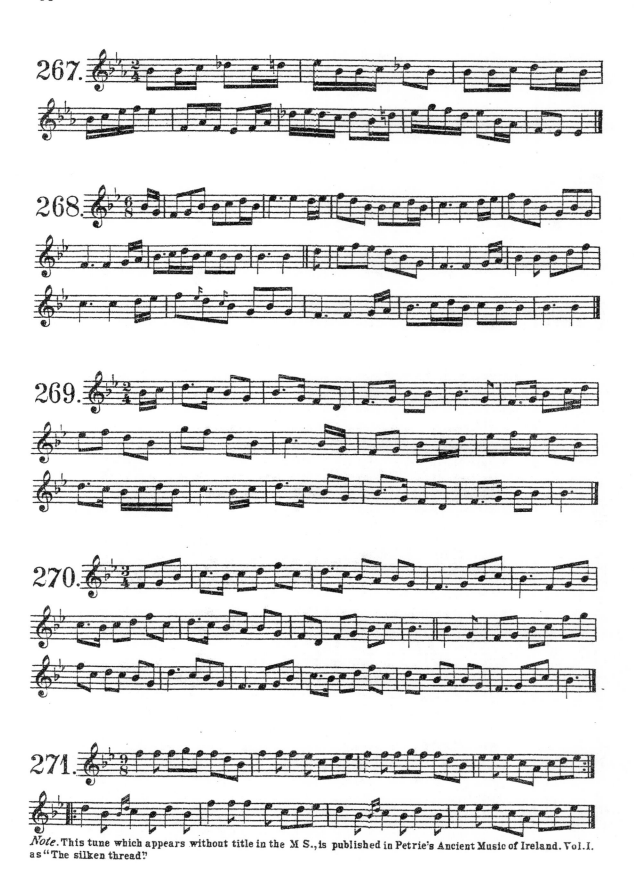

Note. This tune which appears without title in the M S., is published in Petrie's Ancient Music of Ireland. Vol. I. as "The silken thread."

272. Andante. From Frank Keane. 1858.

Arran More tune. From Pat. Mullin, 8th Sep. 1857.
273. Andante.

Note. The small notes are variants in another setting (which is otherwise identical.)
From Mary O'Mally, 7th Sep. 1857.

Arran More tune. From Peter Cooke, 9th Sep. 1857.
274. Allegretto.

Note. This tune appears again, but without source or date.

Arran More tune.
275. Andante.

68

Arran air.

From Mary O'Malley, 7th Sep. 1857.

Andante.

276.

Arran air.

277.

Note. The accidentals seem very questionable. See No 324. Ed.

Arran More.

From James Gill.

Allegretto.

278.

Arran More tune.

From Mary O'Donohoe, 13th Sep. 1857.

Allegro moderato.

279.

70

From the Chief Baron, set by him from a fisher at Kilrush.

283.

From Wᵐ Carleton.

284.

From Wᵐ Carleton.

285.

Name unknown.

286.

Allegretto.

From Mrs Close.

287.

Allegro.

From J. S. Close.

288.

72

At length I crossed the Ferry.   from Bondsglen C.º Derry.

Allegretto.

289.

The scalded poor Boy.   from P.W. Joyce, Esq.

290.

The scalded poor Boy.   from Mr. Joyce.

Andante.

291.

Note: Variant of preceding. Ed.

The Tumbling down Teady's acre. King's C.º   from M.ʳ M.ᶜDermott.

292.

The Barley Grain.   from James Quane, a farmer, Coolfree C⁰ Limerick.

Allegro.

293.

D.C.

The Barley Grain.   from James Quane, a farmer, Coolfree C⁰ Limerick.

294.

Note: Variant of preceding.

Shins about the Fire.   from D.H.Kelly Esq., Castle Kelly.

Allegro.

295.

74

There is a long house at the top of the village.

from Patrick Mullen, Arranmore Sep.18.1857.

Andante.

296.

Street Ballad

Set in Kevin's Port, Dublin 19ᵗʰ June 1852.

297.

Milking time is over.

from the Collection of J.E.Pigott,Esq.,set by Forde.

298.

75

If I'm alive in Ireland.   from Peter Cooke, Arranmore, 9th Sep. 1857.

299. Andante.

Dear Aileen I'm going to leave you.   a Co Cork tune. from P. MacDowell, Esq.

300.

Darby O'Dun.   form O'Neill's MS. 1787.

301.

The Maids of Mourne Shore.   Set in the Co of Derry, 1834.

302.

In the Month of June, when all flowers bloom.   set in the Co. of Derry, 1834.

303.

The Plains of Mayo.   set from Anne Buckley, Claddagh, 1839.

304.

The Eagle's whistle.   (P. Carew's MS.)

305.

The Eagle's whistle.   from P. Carew's MSS.

306.

A variant of preceding.

Biddy, I'm not jesting.   set from Paddy Coneely.

Moderato.

307.

The variants are indicated by the small notes. Ed.

The Kerry Boys.   from P. Carew's MS.

308.

I am a poor Maid that's crossed by my friends.   set by W. Forde.

309.

+) Another version has D♮ here. Ed.

Patrick Sarsfield.

310.

The lament for Sarsfield.

311.

och oh   och och oh oh

78

Modern air on the same theme.

312.

I have two brothers and they are in the army, The one of them's in Cork and the other's in Killarny
With my ri-fol-de - lay.

Lord send the French without delay. '98 Song.   set by W. Forde.

313.

Lord send the French without delay. '98 Song.   P. Conneely.

314.

A variant of the preceding.

Here's a health to the young man, runs most in my mind.

Andante.   P. McDowell Esq. W. Forde and J. E. Pigott, Esq.

315.

Well done, cries she, Brave Donnelly.

316.

Stately Sarah. **Allegretto.**

317.

The Groves by Jackson.

Allegro moderato.

318.

+ *Note*. The C is Petrie's. The whole tune ought probably to be in $\frac{2}{4}$ time, like the following, No 319. Ed.

The Groves: called also The drunken sailor.

A variant of the preceding.

The wind that shakes the barley.   as in O'Neill's collection.

The wind that shakes the barley. As in Mr. Pigott's collection 2nd setting.

Obtained from S.O'Daly.

Oh fair John my love. from Mary O'Flaherty, alias Delane. Arran Sept. 10th 1857.

Variants.

The enchanted valley. set from Mary O'Malley, Arran More Sep. 9th 1857.

Andante.

Note: Variant of O fair John my love.

See "The enchanted valley." +) from Peter Mullin, Arranmore 8th Sept. 1857.

+)Petrie's note.

Beautiful Molly Mc Keon.

Set in the Co of Derry.

*)Another version has G♮ here

My love what is the reason you cannot fancy me.

*)Another version has G♮

We'll drink to the health of Keenan. set from Mary O'Donohoe, Arran-More, 19. Sep. 1857.
Allegretto.

*)Another version has G♮ here

The Maid of sweet Gurteen.

From the Dublin Ballad Singers.

Andante.

328.

+ So written by Petrie. Probably equal to a pause. Ed.

The Maid of Sweet Gurteen.

From P. Carew's M. S.

329.

A variant of the preceding.

Where, were you all the day my own pretty Boy.

P. W. Joyce, Esq.

330.

*)Variant.

I'll make for my Bridegroom a grassy green Pillow.

P. W. Joyce, Esq.

331.

O' Coghlan has a glen.　　　　　　set from Mary O' Donohoe. Arran-more. Sep. 9th 1857.

332.

(Chorus).

Open the door my love, do.

Andante.

333.

*)Another version has G♮

The Nore is long.　　　　　　A. Kilkenny ballad air. From J. G. A. Prim, Esq.

Andante.

334.

*)Another version has B♭ in these places.

Far, far, down in the South of Luidach.　　　　　set from M. O' Donohoe. Arranmore 13 Sep. 1857.

Allegretto.

335.

Alas, that I'm not a Frechaun on the Mountain Side. set from M. O'Donohoe, Arran~more 1857.

Andante.

Note. Title also given by Petrie as, "Alas that I am not a Freechaun on this Mountain Side." Ed.

The Banks of the sweet. Barrow.   set in the Co. of Derry, 1834.

The Banks of Barrow.   second setting from the late T. Davis Esq.

The sweet Barrow.

339.

The one horned Cow.

340.

The one-horned Cow.
As obtained by J. E. Pigott, Esq. from Miss O'Connell of Grena.

Second setting.

341.

The one - horned Cow.

Third Setting from O'Neill's MS.

342.

The Dusty Miller.

343.

The Dusty Miller.   Second setting.

344.

Far, far beyond yon Mountains.   C⁰ Tyrone from the Rev. James Mease.

345.

Original Melody of "S! Patrick was a Gentleman,"   as played by the Irish Militia Bands.

346.

The new Tenpenny.

from P. Carew's M. S.

347.

Horace the Rake.

set from F. Keane.

348. Allegretto.

I thought my heart had broke asunder, when I thought on Reilly I left on shore.

349. Andante.

O' Reilly's Delight.

350.

John O' Reilly.   From Mr MacDowell Mar. 1859.

351. Andante.

The Jug of Punch, A Reel.   From P. Carew's MSS.

352.

The Jug of Punch.   An air formed on that called Brigid astore.
I spied a thrush on yonder bush, And the song she sang was a jug of punch.

353.

Note. This tune appears also with the beginning of the bar marked after the first quaver. Ed.

The merry old Woman.

354.

Old Women's Money.

Second setting of above

355.

The merry old Woman.

356.

The red-haired Man's Wife - as sung in Munster.

357.

The red-haired Man's Wife.

From P. MacDowell Esq.

358.

A variant of the preceding.

The red - haired Man's Wife.   From P. Carew's MSS.

359.

Another setting of the preceding.

The roving Pedlar.   The original air of the Boys of Kilkenny.

360.

This tune is also known as "The red - haired man's wife." Ed.

Down the Hill.   From P. Carew's MS.

361.

*Another version has F♮ here.

The Gaol of Clonmell.

from P. Carew's M.S.

*)Another version has G♮.

Numbers I've courted and kissed in my time.

Andante.

The Newry Prentice Boy.

from P. MacDowell, Esq.

Allegro moderato.

The Death of General Wolfe.

Rathmullen, Co.Donegal, from the Rev. J. Mease.

Andante con spirito.

*)Sic. Ed.

With my Dog and my Gun.

366.

Sprightly Kitty.

O' Neill's M. S.

367.

The green Bushes.

from P. Carew's M.S.S.

Andante.

368.

See "The Capa danig." Petrie.

The green Bushes.

from Mr. Fitzgerald.

Andante.

369.

2nd Setting.

The green Bushes.

Co. of Cork. from P. Mac. Dowell, Esq.

Andante.

370.

*) Another version has G♮.
✛) Another version has F♮. Variant of preceding.

94

Oh, girl of the golden tresses

set from P. Mullin, Arran - More 10th Sep. 1857.

Andante.

371.

Rossaveel. The old form of the Flowers of Edinburgh.

set from Mary O'Donoghoe,
Arran - More, Sep. '57.

372.

Larry O'Gaff.

373.

Donnell O'Daly.   From Mary O' Flaherty, Arran- More 11th Sep. '57.

374.

Tommy Regan.   From John Dulhanny (Costello Bay) at Arran - More 10th Sep. 1857.

375.

*) Another version has C♯ here.

Sweet Innismore - as sung in Connemara.   From Mary O' Malley, Arran- More, 7th Sep. 1857.

376.

I will raise my sail black, mistfully in the morning.   From Mary O' Malley and James Gill.
Arran - More 8th Sep. 1857.

377.

96

Pretty Mary Bilry.   from Mary O'Malley, Arranmore 7th Sept.1857.
Andante quasi Allegro.

378.

Incomplete in the MS. Another version supplies the missing bars. Ed.

The good ship Planet.   from Pat Folan. Arranmore 8th Sep.1857.

379.

With her dog and her gun.   A Mayo tune.
Andante.

380.

Now I am tired and wish I was at home.

381.

The flowing locks of my brown maid. set in Mayo by Forde.

382.

+)Another version has B♭ here.

The little red lark of the Mountain. An Erris tune from P. Coneely.

383.

The little red lark of the Mountain. from the County Armagh.

384.

98

The Phelim Mountains.

385.

Note. This tune also appears with its title in Gaelic. Ed.

Hear me you that's looking for a wife.

386.

Leave that as it is. Allegretto.

387.

+)Another version has F♮ here.
Another version of this tune has the title "Let us leave that as it is."

'Twas on the first of May, brave boys.

From Rev J. Meaze(sic) Rathmullen.

388.

Chorus.

The merchant's daughter.   From P. MacDowell Esq. From Skull.

389.

The bright dawn of day.   From Skull. P. MacDowell Esq.

390.

*) Another version has E♭ here.

The brave Irish lad.   From Tuam P. MacD.

Moderato.

391.

Captain Slattery.   From F. Keane.

Allegretto.

392.

100

Leather bags Donnel.

From P. Carew's MSS.

393.

The cutting of the hay.

From P. Mac Dowell Esq.

394.

The Rambler from Clare.*)

Andante.

From P. Mac Dowell Esq.

395.

*) O' Connell! Note by Petrie.

The Mill Stream, a County of Cork reel.

From P. Carew's MSS.

396.

Take her out and air her-a Cork Reel · · From P. Carew's MSS.

397.

Coadys' dream.

398.

The King and the Tinker. · From O' Neill's Collection 1787.

399.

*)Another version has E♮ in these places.

Miss Goulding - by Carolan. · From John O' Daly's MSS.

400.

102

I shall leave this country and go along with you to
wander under the arches of the blossomed woods.

From P.J.O'Reilly Esq.

Allegretto.

401.

The lovers complaint.

From O'Neill's collection 1787.

402.

Clout the Caldron.

From O'Neill's collection 1787.

403.

The first of May.

404.

Another version of this tune has no dotted notes. See 388.

The ship that I command.

405.

÷)2 versions have D here and one has E.

Rodney's Glory.

406.

Index says "as sung in the county of Derry".
+Another version has D♭here.

Rodney's glory as sung in the county of Londonderry.

407.

King Cormac and the Lericaun.

408.

MacGuire's Kick _a March.

409.

104

Maguire's Kick.

The rebels' march in 1798.

410.

Air, name unknown.

411.

The mountain road.

412.

Chasing the hare down the hill.

443.

Note: Petrie calls this tune the same as the jig "The humours of Milltown." Ed.

Bessy of Dromore.

414.

Chorus.

Bessy of Dromore.

415.

A Variant of the preceding.

The four seasons.

416.

The Ploughman and the Taylor.   Galway Aug. 28th 1840.

417.

106

Red Regan and the Nun.

Andante.

418.

Red Regan and the Nun.

419.

Red Regan and the Nun.

420.

A Variant of the preceding.

The Maiden-Ray.   Set in the Cladagh Galway Aug. 28th 1840.

421.

The banks of Claudy.

422.

+)Another version has C♮ here.

The Banks of Claudy.

as set by Forde from Mr. Pigot's MSS.

423.

N.B. Two other sets by Forde are in the minor.

Curly Locks.

Andante.

424.

The battle of the Roe, by Gillan.

425.

108

The battle of the Roe.

426.

A variant of the preceding.

The battle of the Roe.

427.

Another variant.

The battle of the Roe, by Gillan.

428.

Another version.

Gramachree, but I love you well.

429.

In another version the bar lines begin as follows:

etc. etc.

Adieu, my lovely Peggy.

430.

'Twas on a Summer evening.

431.

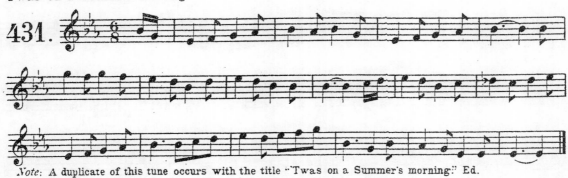

Note: A duplicate of this tune occurs with the title "'Twas on a Summer's morning." Ed.

'Twas on a Summer's evening.

M! Joyce, from Joseph Martin.

Allegretto.

432.

Air, name unknown.

433.

I am a bold defender.

434.

+)Another version has E♮ here.

110

On the green stubble in harvest.

As sung by Margaret Callan.

435.

✢ Another version has G♭ here.

Yesterday morning as I walked alone.

436.

Yesterday evening as I walked alone.

437.

Variant of preceding.

Ancient Irish Air.

Sung as the Plaint in the Parish of Dungiven.

438.

✢ Two other versions omit this bar.

The winter it is past.

439.

Known also as "The Curragh of Kildare." Ed.

The drums are beating.

440.

From J. Bridgford.

441.

The mother cries Boys do not take my dear   from me - For if yes

do my ghost will hant yes Love Fare - well. - - - - - - - -

The drums are   beating   and   colours   flying

Variant of preceding.

The hornless cow, - or the brown ewe (a private still.)✚

442.

Two other versions of this begin
with the bar lines thus.

✚ Set by Forde from the people of Glen Farne. From J. Pigott, Esq.

I'd cross the world over with you Johnny Doyle.

443.

Kitty gone a milking.

444.

The lover's lament. From Galway.

P. Mac Dowell, Esq.

Andante.

445.

Paddy Brown.

446.

From P. Carew's M.S. see the tune "Kitty alone".(Petrie's note.)

Molly Asthoreen.

Rather slow.

447.

✠ Another version omits the ♮s in these places.

The northern road to Tralee.

448.

An ancient Clare march. ✠ Another version has no flat in these two places. Ed.

I wish I was a fisherman living upon the hill of Howth.

449.

"All alive", from Tighe's old M.S. book.   "Your welcome to Waterford".

450.

The brown thorn, correctly set.

451.

I once loved a boy.

452.

cresc.

Note: This title occurs again, Nº 471, with a different tune. Ed.

Last night I dreamt of my own true love.

Andante   Mr. Joyce, from Peggy Cudmore.

453.

✝ Another version has F♯

The dewy morning.

Andante: From Mr. Mac Dowell.

454.

See No. 447 "Molly Asthoreen."

I am a poor maiden. my fortune proved bad.

Mr. Joyce, from Peggy Cudmore.

Come all you maids where'er you be.

From Mr. Joyce.

The moving bog – a Munster Reel.

From MS. Music Book.

The Pullet. A Munster Reel.

From MS. Music Book.

The Shanavest and Corovoth, a faction tune.

459. Andante.   Mr. Joyce from his grandmother, aged 90.

I lost my love.   From Frank Keane.

460. Allegro moderato.

When you go to a battle.   Mr. Joyce, from Joseph Martin.

461. Allegretto.

CHORUS.

Toss the Feathers. A Clare Reel.   From Frank Keane.

462.

+Another version has a ♯ in these places.

Come all y'united - Irishmen, and listen unto me.

Mr. Joyce, from J. Martin and P. Cudmore.

Allegretto.

463.

✚ Another version has a ♯ in these places.
(✚) Another version has a ♮ here.

Come all united Irishmen and listen unto me.

Set by Mr. Joyce from J. Martin.

Con spirito.

464.

How deep in love am I.

465.

The strolling mason.

Andante.

466.

Note: Another setting of this occurs with title in Gaelic. Ed.

118

Then up comes the captain & boatswain.   From Mr. Joyce.

467.

The far away wedding.   Mr. Joyce, from Connor Hannan, near Kildorrery. Co. of Cork.

468.

Oh love it is a killing thing.   From Mr. Joyce.

469.

My honest dear neighbour I ne'er killed your cat.

470.

I once loved a boy.   set by Mr. Joyce from Peggy Cudmore.

471.

O'Neill's riding.   From O'Neill's collection, 1787.

472.

The Breeches on.   From O'Daly's Kilrush MS.

473.

Same as "The Irish Lad." (Petrie's note.) See Nᵒˢ 586 and 989. Ed.

Mary do you fancy me.   as sung by an old Connaught beggarman in Gʳᵗ Britain St.

Gaily.

474.

120

The blackberry blossom.

Reel time.

475.

The scolding wife.

476.

Humours of last night. Jig.

From O'Neill's collection.

477.

When the cock crows it is day.

From O'Neill's collection.

478.

Clonmell lassies.

From O'Neill's collection.

479.

Air, name unknown.

480.

Note: A variant of № 255.

Katty Nowlan.

From P. Coneely.

481.

Catty Nowlan.

Catty Nowlan.

482.

The strawberry blossom.

483.

The strawberry blossom. A Reel.

from P. Carew's M S.

484.

Air, name unknown.

Mr Joyce from his brother Mr M. J.

485.

Chorus.

Note: A slight variant of No 224.

The son of O'Reilly.

486.

Hunt the squirrel⁺- as in the Dancing-master 17th Ed. 1721.

487.

⁺ an Irish March.

I am asleep and don't wake me.

488.

Roscommon Air.

489.

124

The monks of the screw.

From Wᵐ H. Curran, Esq.

490.

Once I was at a Nobleman's wedding.

as sung by Margaret Callan.

491.

Once I was at a Nobleman's wedding.

Andante.

From Mr. Fitzgerald.

492.

Once I was invited to a nobleman's wedding.

From Mr. Joyce.

493.

A variant of Nº 491.

"Once I was at a Nobleman's wedding." Learnt in the County of Mayo.   From Dr Kelly.

Once I was invited to a noble wedding.

Air, name unknown.   From Mr J. S. Close.

I wish the French would take them.

The Maid of Timahoe.

498.

C f. "As I roved out one morning." Nº 657. Ed.

O' Flinn. by Carolan.

499.

Note: See Nºs 871 to 876. Ed.

Pretty Sally.

500.

This tune also occurs in **4/4** time. Ed.

The Petrie Collection of Irish Music.

PART II

The gamest toast.

501.

We brought the summer with us.

502.

Of all the fish that's in the sea, the **Herring is king** the herring is king. Sing

thuga - mur fein an samh - ra linn'tis we have brought the sum - mer in

The storm is o'er 'tis calm again; We're safe on shore from the raging main, Sing

thu gamar fein an samh - -ra linn,'tis we have brought the sum - mer in.

+ **Probably E. Another Version in E minor is in Petrie's printed collection. Ed.**

Lilibulero.

503.

128

This fine old melody appears in the Dancing Master 4th Edition as "Grey goose Fair," thus: -

504.

I have travelled France & Germany.

505.

Allan's return.

506.

I rise in the morning with my heart full of woe. _

A Cavan air.

507.

Known also as "Coola Shore". Ed.

Down among the ditches, oh.

508.

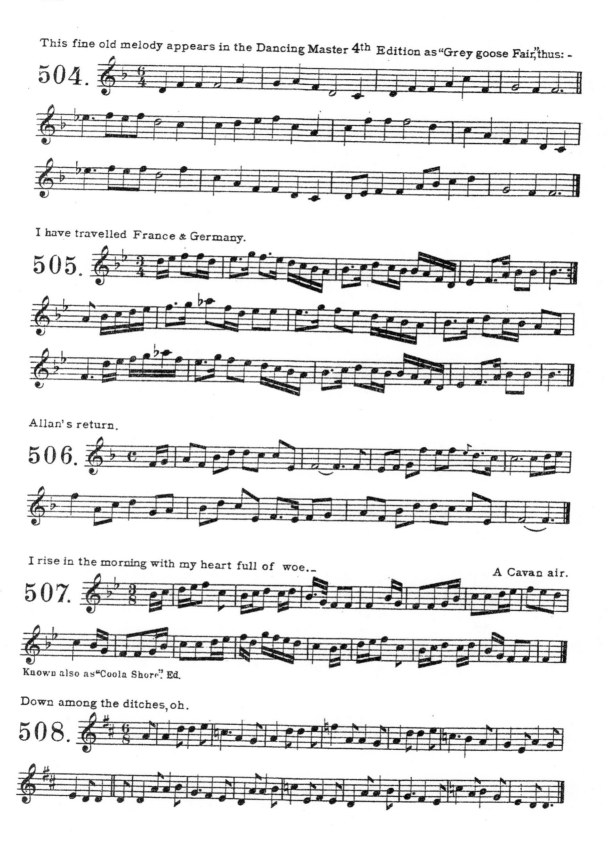

My wife is sick and like to die, oh dear what shall I do.

509.

Rise up young William Reilly.

510.

Rise up my lovely Molly.

From Mr. Fitzgerald.

511.

Kitty O' Hea.

Donegal tune
From Mr. Allingham.

512.

130

Kitty Magee.

513.

Kitty's wishes.

Allegro moderato.

from Mr Mac Dowell Dec. 1859.

514.

The heart of my Kitty soon turns to me.

515.

Oh my love she was born in the North country wide.

Note. See the variant setting of this (in the major) under its Gaelic title. Ed.

Our sails were unfurled.

Dear Rose.

Along the Mourne shore.

Hold your tongue.

✛ Another version has C♯ here. Ed.

My song I will finish, her name's Miss Jane Innis.

521.

Tatter the road.

522.

Tear the callies.

523.

Molly my jewel.

524.

Molly my jewel.

525.

Note. A variant of the preceding. Ed.

I am a rover.

526.

An old man he courted me, will you love, can you love:
An old man he courted me, take me as I am.

Moderato.

527.

Note. Another version repeats the 1ˢᵗ four bars. Ed.

An old man he courted me.

from Mʳ Joyce.

Andante.

528.

134

The young wife and her old husband - Dialogue. C? of Monaghan Air.   Byrne.Hooper.April 6.42.

Allegro.

529.

Andante.

+)*Note*. This title appears again in Gaelic and English but with a different tune. Ed.

Oh what shall I do with this silly old man.

530.

Ne'er wed an old man.   C? Limerick. Mr. Joyce.

Andante.

531.

How do you like her for your wife.   From Mr. Joyce.

532.

Note. cf "Cousin Frog" N? **647**. Ed.

On a long long summer's day.

From M$^{rs.}$ Close.

533.

Chorus.

My store is short and my journey is long.

534.

"Oh were I king of Ireland".

From Mrs. Close.

535.

My love she is far sweet—er than an—y flow'r that blows, the lil—ly or car—

na—ti—on, the pink or blistering rose. Her love—ly form and fea——tures with

such a graceful mien, oh love it is a kill—ing thing, Did you ev—er feel the pain?

But, be it so, or be it not,
Or be it but a chance,
The very first time I saw my love,
She struck me in a trance.

Her ruby lips and sparkling eyes
They so bewitched me,
Oh were I king of Ireland
Queen of it she should be.

I'll be a good boy and do so no more.

From the county of Cavan.

536.

136

The good boy.

From P. Carew's M S S.

Andante.

537.

The fair girl.

538.

The Blessington maid.

From Mr. Pigot's M S.

Andante.

539.

The girl I love.

From P. Carew's M S S.

540.

Note. Petrie marks this "bad set." See Nọ 949 and compare with Nọ 959 Ed.

The wearied lad.

Set by Lord Rosmore from P. Coneely 1843.

Allegro.

541.

I love a woman." or "The dwarf of the glens."

from Mr. Pigot's M S.

Andante.

542.

138

The rushy glen.

From Mr Pigot's MS.

543.

The fairy troop.

Andante.

From Mr Pigot's MS.

544.

The old Astrologer.

From Mr Patrick Joyce.

545.

The Gobby O.

546.

Note. This tune appears in the manuscript with the signature as above, but Petrie printed it(in "Ancient music of Ireland") without the sharp. Ed.

The Enniskilling Dragoon.

From P. Carew's MSS.

Note. This tune appears to be a variant of "Skillet dubh." Ed.

The rocky road.

? Ed.

The high road to Kilkenny.

From Mrs Close.

The song of Una. Very ancient.

140

Second set.

From old M S. given me by J. Hardiman.

551.

The song of the streams.

552.

The first day of spring.

From Mr Joyce.

553.

The Harmony of May.

From Miss Ross.

554.

The summer is come and the grass is green.   Mr Joyce from Michael Hennesy, Kilfinnane.

555.

Note. Another version has C♮ in these places. Ed.

The Praises of Downhill.

556.

The downhill of Life.   From Mr Pigot's M S.

557.

The Belfast Mountain.   From Mr P. Mac Dowell R. A. March 59

558.

142

The Mountain high - a tune of Bonds glen.

Parish of Camber.

559.

The top of Sweet Dunmul.

560.

The borders of sweet Coole Hill.

A. Cavan air.

561.

The Hill without grass.

From Teige Mac Mahon.

562.

The forlorn virgin.

563.

The night of the fun.

564.

The Connemara Wedding.

565.

The rejoicement of the Fian Ladies - an Ossianic air.

566.

The Lobster pot.

From F. Keane.

Allegro moderato.

567.

The ship of Patrick Lynch.

568.

The seas are deep.

569.

The dangers of the sea.

570.

The foundering of the boat, in Lough Derag, Sunday the 12ᵗʰ of July 1795.

571.

The praises of Rathfriland.

572.

The groves of Blackpool, or the Cove of Cork.

The Black joke, as in an old Kerry MS.

From Father Walsh.

The white Rock.

The green Flag.

146

The yellow Horse.

From an old MS

577.

Note. This title appears again in Gaelic with a different tune. Ed.

The yellow bustard, a county of Leitrim air.

578.

The Black Phantom.

From the Revd Father Walsh.

579.

The song of the Ghost.

580.

Note. ✦ Another harmonised version of this air has an F♯ here. Both sharps are probably interpolated. Ed.

The soft Deal Board.

From Father Walsh.

581.

The soft deal bed.

A Munster air.

582.

The little Cuckoo of Ard Patrick.

From Father Walsh.

Allegro.

583.

The flannel jacket.

From P. Carew's MSS.

584.

148

The Pullet and the Cock.

From Frank Keane.

585.

Fine.

D.C.

The Irish boy.

From my Father.

586.

Note. A slight variant of No 989. See "The Breeches on" No 473. Ed.

The Irish Boree.

From "The Dancing Master" 17th Edition London 1721.

587.

The Irish trot.

From the 17th edition of the Dancing Master London 1721.

588.

The Juice of the Barley.

F. T. Mac Mahon.

589.

H. 3279

The sprightly Widow.   From Mr. Pigot's MS.

590.

The peevish child.   by Jerome Dingenan.

591.

The Gossip.   Mrs. Close.

592.

The Parish girl.   set about 1800 by Danl Mc Hourigan.

593.

150

The funny Taylor.

From Mr Joyce.

594.

The Bailiff's one daughter.

595.

The Dairy girl.

From. T. Davis.

596.

The Dairy - Maid's wish.

Allegro

597.

The Coolin, as sung in Clare.

From Taig Mac Mahon.

598.

The old Coolin.

599. Moderato.

The Squire.

600.

Chorus.

+ The MS. has neither clef nor siguature. Ed.

The handsome sportsman.

601.

The sons of Fingal.

602.

152

The Plough Boy.

County of Leitrim from Lord Dunraven Jan. 1860.

Moderato

603.

The Hurling boys. A very popular tune of the King's County.

Allegretto.

604.

The croppy boy.

From Mr Joyce.

605.

The croppy boy, different air.

606.

The wee bag of Praties.

607.

The blooming lily.

608.

The garden of daisies.

609.

cf. Nº 20 Ed.

The garden of Daisies, a Kerry tune.

610.

The Bird alone.

From Mr. J. Keane's book. Kilrush.

Andante.

611.

The Bird alone.

612.

The Dove.

613.

Called also "When she answered me, her voice was low." Ed.

The Dove.

Andante.

614.

The Humours of Caledon.

615.

The Humours of Maam.

Allegro.

616.

Note. The variants are supplied from two other versions of this tune. Ed.

The Humours of Jerpoint.

617.

The Eilan.

From Iverk. The Revᵈ Mr. Graves.

618.

The Sigh.

619.

156

The old woman lamenting her purse.

620.

The white breasted boy.

Mrs Close.

621.

Note. A variant of Nos. 72 and 140. Ed.

I'll make my love a breast of glass.

From Bet Skilling.

622.

The pearl of the white breast.

623.

Called also "The Snowy-breasted Pearl." Ed.

The pearl of the fair pole of hair.

624.

Shamus O'Thomush – or James Melvin.(A Jacobite Air).

From Mrs.Clos

625.

Jacobite Air - from Kerry.

From Father Walsh.

Andante.

626.

Jacobite Air.

From Father Walsh.

627.

158

Oh, Love, 'tis a cold frosty night, and I am covered with snow.   From R. Fitzgerald.

628.

I'd range the world over with my own Johnny Doyle.   From Forde.

629.

Note A slight variant of N⁰ 443. Ed.

Johnny Doyle.   From Mr. Joyce.

630.

There's one thing be - tween I think it a - miss

He goes to meeting and I go to Mass I'll go to Mass a - long with +

and think it no toil For I'd range the world over with my own Johnny Doyle.
+ *Sic.* The words are not written carefully beneath the notes. Ed.

Poor Catholic brother.
Very Slow.

631.

Oh shrive me, father.
Andantino.

632.

One Sunday after Mass.

633.

Blow the candle out.

634.

When I am dead and my days are over,
Come Molly astoreen and lay me down.

From Mr Joyce.

635.

N.B. A similar tune (in the minor) appears under the title "Molly Asthoreen" No 447 Ed.

O Mary Asthore.

Allegretto.

636.

When first I came to the county Cavan.

From Joseph Hughes.

637. Andante.

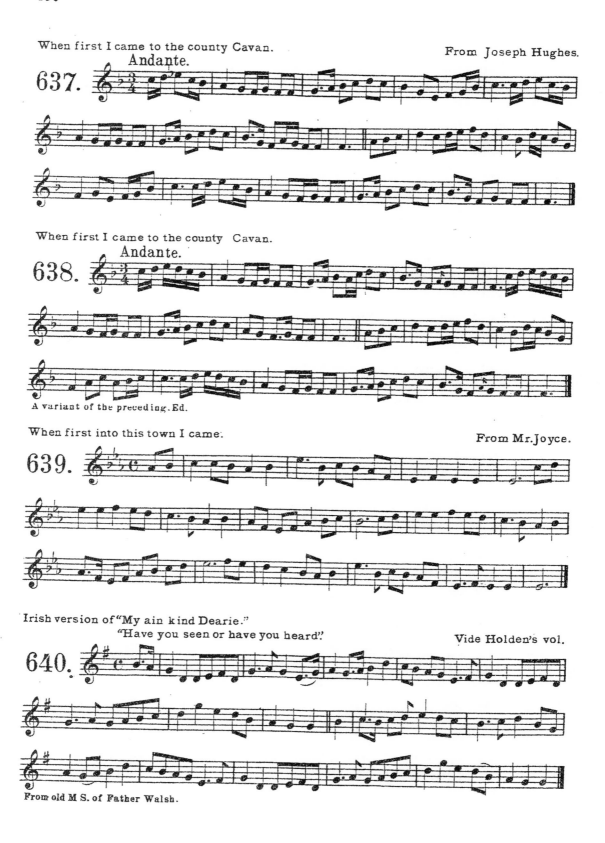

When first I came to the county Cavan.

638. Andante.

A variant of the preceding. Ed.

When first into this town I came.

From Mr. Joyce.

639.

Irish version of "My ain kind Dearie."
"Have you seen or have you heard."

Vide Holden's vol.

640.

From old M S. of Father Walsh.

Same air. "My ain kind dearie" - "Sweet Innisfallen" and Lover's "Widow Machree."

641.

As sung by Mr Joyce's father.

Reynardine.

From Father Walsh's M S.

642.

Reynardine.

From a ballad singer at Rathmines. Nov. 1852

643.

A variant of the preceding. Ed.

Reynard on the mountain high.

Co. Tyrone, from Lord Dunraven. Jan. 1860

644.

A variant of N.º 642. Ed.

162

The fox went out of a moonlight night. Set in the Cladagh.

645.

The fox went out of a moonlight night.

646.

A variant of the preceding. Ed.

Cousin frog went out to ride. Fa lee linkin' laddy Oh.

647.

Note: The M S. has neither clef nor signature. Ed.

Nelly, I'm afraid your favour I'll not gain.   From Father Walsh's M S.

648.

The Gorey Caravan.

From Mary Hackett. P. Joyce.

649.

I cannot do without her — I will find her if I can.
My curse attend the driver—Oh he drives the Caravan.

"Search all the world over."

From T. Davis (N)

650.

lento *pp*

Come sit down beside me my own heart's delight.

From the Bennad glens.

651.

Lough Erne's shore.

From Miss Ross.

652.

164

Second of the above air.   From Miss Ross.

653.

When you are sick, 'tis tea you want.

654.

Who told you these false stories.   From Mr R. Fitzgerald.

655.

Consider well all you pretty fair maids.   From Mr R. Fitzgerald.

656.

As I roved out one morning.

From Mr Joyce b.b.p.35

657. Andante.

A variant of N°. 498.
Note. Petrie adds title in pencil "The maid of Timahoe." Ed.

As I walked out one morning, I heard a dismal cry.

From Mr R. A. Fitzgerald.

658. Spiritoso.

As I walked out one evening (county of Wexford)

From Mr R. A. Fitzgerald.

659. Andante.

One evening of late as I roved out in state.

From Mr Joyce p. 14

660. Andante.

÷ Another version has E♮ here. Ed.

166

As I walked over the county Cavan.

Andante.

From Js Mac Closkey. Dungiven.

661.

One evening fair as I roved out.

From Mr Joyce.

662.

As I was walking one morning in May.

Andante.

From P. Coneely.

663.

As I strayed out on a foggy morning in harvest.

664.

As I walked out yesterday evening.

665.

As I went a walking one morning in Spring.

P. W. Joyce, Esq.

666.

As through the woods I chanced to roam.

From Mr. Joyce p.20.

667.

The rambling boy.

Badly set in Bunting v.3.

668.

Carolan's draught.

669.

From Father Walsh. M S.

Carolan's Cottage.

670.

Andante.

From P. Carew's M S S.

Separation of soul and body.

671.

Attributed to Carolan

The reading made easy.

from Father Walsh's M.S.

"I courted lovely Sally."

from Father Walsh's M.S.

I courted my darling at the age of nineteen. Set in the county of Derry.

Never despise an old friend.

from Miss Ross.

In comes great Buonaparte with forty thousand men.

from Mr. Joyce.

+ Another version has G♯ here Ed.

Glencoe.

from R. Fitzgerald.

"It was an old Beggarman"-as sung in Donegal

from Mr. Allingham.

It was an old Beggarman weary and wet
And down by the fi-re side he sat.
He threw down his bags and his broken staff,
And merrily he did sing.

My dear said he if I were as free,
As when I first came to this countrie
I'd dress you up. all beggarly.
And away with me you should gang-oh.

Chorus: With his pipe in his jaw,
And his jaw full of smoke,
And the dribbles hung down
To the breast of his cloak
His bag on his back
And his staff in his hand,
He's a jolly old Beggarman-oh.

The Duke of Aberdeen (see "The Beggarman" in Bunting.)

from P. Carew's M SS.

The blind beggar of the glen.

set by J. E. Pigot, Esq.
from Mr. Flatley's singing.

680.

Remember the poor.

681.

As sung by the Dublin Ballad
singers, 1810.

Remember the pease straw.

682.

David Foy—as sung by the Dublin street ballad singers, for the last fifty years at least.

683.

Note. A variant of the preceding. Ed.

172

The blind man's dream.

Allegretto.

684.

+ Another version has.

My love he is tall although he is young. A Wexford air.

from Mr. R. Fitzgerald.

685.

The suit of green.

set in Carlow County by Mr. Watson.

686.

+ Another version has D♭ here.
Note. This tune appears again in F major, with the time –signature 𝄴. Ed.

As Jimmy and Nancy one evening were straying.

687.

Heigh ho!my Nancy oh–as sung by James Moylan, gardener.

From T.B.

688.

Heigh ho my Nancy oh!
Heigh ho my Nancy oh!
Yonder there's my mother the Queen
And the swan she swam so bonny oh!

Nancy the pride of the east.

From Father Walsh M.S.

689.

Note. Petrie says there is "a more than usual agreement" between the different versions of this tune.
The melody he prints under this title is different to the above. Ed.

A lady in Pensylvania Lovely Nancy you'll be.

690.

tr

174

The Deserter. As sung in the county of Carlow.   From Mr. Watson.

691.

Note. Another version of this tune occurs without the repetition of the third four-bar phrase. Ed.

Perhaps you and I will be judged in one day.

692.

Another version has no ♭ here. Ed.

Oh Johnny dearest Johnny, what dyed your hands and cloaths?
He answered him as he thought fit "by a bleeding at the nose."

693.

The dawning of the day.   From Kate Keane. Dec. 1854.

694.

Note. A variant of the preceding. Ed.

Ballymoe.   From J.E. Pigot. Esq.

695.

Note. The two "trs" and the ♭ in bar 13 are supplied from another version. Ed.

A Waterford boat song.   From Mr. O'Kelly.

696.

I have no desire for mirth.

697.

They say my love is dead.   From Scullun a Fiddler, Bellaghy

698.

I griev for my lover in secret.

699

+ B♮ ? But probably should be B♭ and C♮. Ed.

My lover is fled, my heart is sore.

From P.J.O' Reilly, Esq.

700.

My love will ne'er forsake me.

From P.J.O' Reilly, Esq.
Westport.

701.

Must I be bound and my Love be free.

R. Fitzgerald.

702.

My love is in the house.

A Cork Reel. From Carew's MSS

703.

My love she won't come near me.

From Mr R.A. Fitzgerald.

Andante.

704.

Note. Petrie has in pencil taken out the E♭ of the signature, and added E♭ in bars 2 and 14. Ed.

The Maid I loved dearly has left me behind.

From P. Mac Dowell.

Andante.

705.

I will visit my love on the mountain.

706.

Along with my love I'll go.

From Mr Joyce.

Andante.

707.

178

Along with my love I'll go.

Andante.

From P. Joyce, Esq

708.

Another version of the preceding. Ed.

The Maid of Castle Creagh.

709.

÷Db? Ed.

My Baby on my arm.

710.

The Greeks' victory.

Andante.

From P. Carew's MSS.

711.

Luggelaw.

712.

From P. Carew's M S.

Catha Rony.

713.

A county of Louth air
from James Tighe.

dim.

f

mf

Down by Newcastle shore.

714.

Lady Shearbrook.

715.

Madame Cole.

One of Carolan's finest airs.

716.

Isbel Falsey - or False Isabel, a Manx air.

717.

Cathleen.

Andante.

718.

Eveleen.

Andante.

719.

Fond Chloe, (A queer name for an Irish air.)   from Mr. R. A. Fitzgerald.

720.

Sweet lovely Joan.   from Mr. F. J. Southwell.

721.

Molly fair, that western dame.

722.

Molly Butler.   A County of Clare tune.

723.

182

Molly Bān so fair.

from P. Mac Dowell Esq.

Andante.

724.

Bridget of the mildest smile.

725.

Lovely Anne.

from P. Coneely.

726.

Sally Whelan - a Joyce country tune.

727.

Note. This tune appears again under the title "Sally Phelan"
  The small notes indicate the differences between the two versions. Ed

Scornful Sally.

From Mr Mac Dowell.

728.

Irish setting of "Black eyed Susan."

729.

Sir Ulick Burk, by Carolan.

From Neal's collection.

730.

Father Jack Walsh.

731.

Stewart of Kilpatrick and the daughter of the king of Ine.

732.

Doctor O' Halloran.

From Mrs. Close.

733.

Bold Captain Friney.

In marching time.

From M! Pigot's M S.

734.

Richard O' Bran from the plains of Kildare.

735.

John Dwyre of the Glyn - From an old Kerry M S.

736.

Roddy Mc Curley that was hanged at Tuome Bridge.

737.

A Kerry tune
from Frank Keane.

John Doe.

Allegretto.

738.

Note. Two other versions of this tune will be found under Gaelic titles. See Index Ed.

Bryan Mac Cowall.

Andante.

739.

Rory O'Moore.

From Miss Ross.

Allegro.

740.

Derry Brien.

741.

Note. Petrie's Index adds 'Same as Savourneen Dheelish. Ed.

John the son Darby. Gaily. From P. Coneely. 1843. Rosmore.

742.

Johnny Cox or Johnny of Cockalie. From E. Clements Esq.

Andante con spirito.

743.

Archy Boylan.

744.

Willy Taylor.

745.

Chorus.

188

Michael Molloy.

750.

Mary I die your slave.

751. Moderato.

Oh where are you going Lord Lovel, said she.

752.

He's gone he's gone.✝

753.

✝The title in Petrie's Index is "He's gone, he's gone, young Johnny's gone, will I never see him more."
Note. In the M S. an extra ♮ is added in pencil to the signature. Ed.

The maid of Cooley Shore.

754.

It was in Dublin city.

755.

It was in Dublin city
A city of great fame
Where first my darling Irish boy
A-courting to me came.

Claudy dwelling.

756.

Adieu ye young men of Claudy green.   Set in the Cº of Derry, 1834.

757.

190

Sweet heart you know my mind: or "I have a little trade." A Connaught tune.

758.

Dear Mother he is going, and I know not how to bid him stay.

759.

Andante.

+*Note.* Another version has D♮ here. Ed.

Dear Mother he is going, and I know not how to bid him stay.

760.

Andante.

A variant of the preceding. Ed.

Note. +Another variant has this group of notes thus.

My parents gave me good advice.

From P. Mac Dowell Esq.

761.

Moderato.

Oh what shall I do, my love is going to be wed.

From Mr. Pigot's M S.

Andante.

762.

Do you hear little girls, take your mother's advice, 'tis the best.

J. Mac Closkey.

Allegretto.

763.

The Advice.

Allegretto.

764.

Early, early, all in the spring.

765.

The lass of Sliabh Bān.

766.

192

Last Saturday night as I lay in my bed.-A white - boy song.   From James O'Reilly Esq.

767.

"Peggy is your head sick" a county of Louth song - also played as a dance and called.
"The long hills of Mourne."

768.

Behind the bush in the garden - as played by Pat Cunningham, a famous W. Meath piper.

769.

If the sea were ink.

770.

As a sailor and a soldier.
From Mr. Joyce.

771.

The soldier's song, "Hark I hear etc."   From the Revd. J. Meaze.   Tyrone & Kilkenny.

772.

Berry Dhoan "The brown oxen" a Manx Air.

773.

Petrie's Note. This air is set in $\frac{2}{4}$ time by Major Wallis.

Where are you going my pretty maid?   County of Cork. From P. Mac Dowell, Esq.

Moderato.

774.

194

Banish misfortune.   From P. Mac Dowell Esq.

Allegretto.

775.

Come tell me in plain.   From Mr. R. A. Fitzgerald.

Andante.

776.

For my breakfast you must get a bird without a bone.   (Wexford) From Mr. R. A. F.

Andante.

777.

For my breakfast etc. (second setting.)   From Mr. Fitzgerald.

Andante.

778.

The bonny light Horseman. (county Wexford.)   From Mr. Fitzgerald.

Andante.

779.

✣ Note. The last two notes have been cut off by the binder and are conjectural. Ed.

In the county of Wexford not far from Tughmon.   From Mr. R. A. Fitzgerald.

Andante spirituoso e marcato.

780.

For I'd rather go (county of Wexford)   From Mr. Fitzgerald.

Andante.

781.

'Tis I your lover. (county of Wexford.)   From Mr. Fitzgerald.

Andante.

782.

196

Ninety-eight Wexford Ballad.
Andante.
783.

From Robert Fitzgerald, Esq Enniscorthy.

'98 Ballad - Co of Wexford.
784.

From R. Fitzgerald.

A second setting of the above air.
785.

Lady Gordon's Minuet.
Andante.
786.

Set by Forde in the Co of Mayo.

Farewell now Miss Gordon.   C? of Wexford, from Mr. Fitzgerald.

Over the mountain.

Dobbin's flow'ry vale.   From M? Joyce b.b. p.36.

Poor old Granua Weal.   From J. M? Closkey. Dungiven.

198

How will I get to the Bedchamber.

Forde.

791.

Crabs in the skillet. From J. Buckley. This tune belongs to the coast of Clare and Limerick.

Mᴿ Joyce.

792.

Some say that I'm foolish and some say I'm wise.

From Mᴿ Pigot's M.S.

793. Andante.

Air to an old English Ballad. Learnt in Mayo.

From Dᴿ Kelly.

794. Andante.

Tune of the old English Ballad "Lord Robert and fair Ellen" as sung in Mayo. From Dr. Kelly.

Jackson's Maid.

Jackson's Maid.

A variant of the preceding. Ed.

Over the water.

by Jackson.

I'am a poor stranger that's far from my home.

The Dublin ballad singers.

I'm a poor stranger that's far from my own.

From Mr Joyce

The lovely sweet banks of the Suir.

From P. Coneely.

The banks of the Suir.

Banks of the Suir.

Note. A variant of the preceding. Ed.

Down by the banks of the sweet Primrose. From Mr Mac Dowell, Decr 1859.

The Banks of the Shannon." From Father Walsh.

Beside the river Loune. From P. Mac Dowell Esq.

Farewell to Lough Rea. From Mr Mac Dowell.

"Van Diemen's Land" A Donegal Melody. From Wm Allingham.

202

The flower of Erin's green shore.

From P. Mac Dowell Esq

809.

My name is Bold Kelly.

From Mr Joyce.

810. Andante.

I wish, I wish, but I wish in vain.

From Frank Keane.

811. Andante.

I wish I were in Drogheda.

812. Allegretto.

Gurty's Frolic – a very old Munster tune.

From M.S. Musick Book.

813.

Allegro.

It is to fair England I'm willing to go.

From Mr Joyce.

814.

Andante.

204

I was one night about Bridgetmas.

Andante.

815.

A woman and twenty of them.   From Mary O'Donohoe. Arran More 13th Sept. 1857.

Andante.

816.

Note. A variant of the preceding. A tune similar to this appears under a Gaelic title. Ed.

I was once sailing by the head.   set from John Dubhana.(Costello bay) Arran - more.

817.

Note. The accidentals in brackets are in a second copy. Ed.

When I go down to the foot of Croagh Patrick.   From Pat. Mullin. Arran More Sept. 1857.

Andante.

818.

Alas that I'm not a little starling bird.   From Pat Mullin. Arran More 10th Sept. 1857.

Andante.

819.

Her skin is like the lily.   From Rev. James Mease, Learned in Tyrone.

Andante.

820.

If all the young maidens were blackbirds and trushes.

Moderato.

821.

The blackbird and the thrush.   Set in the Cladagh. August 28. 1840.

822.

206

In my first proceedings I took rakish ways. Set in C⁰ of Limerick. From M.ʳ MacDowell.

823. **Allegretto.**

O landlady dear, come cheer your heart. A Cavan air.

824. **Allegretto.**

One bottle more.

825. **Andante.**

Chorus.

I was born for sport.

From P. Coneely Jan. 1845 Ros:

826. **Allegretto.**

Mammie will you let me to the Fair.

From P. Coneely Jan. 1845. R.

Moderato.

827.

One evening in June, or Youth and bloom.

From P. Coneely.

Andante.

828.

Cheer up old Hag. Set by Lord Rosmore.

From P. Coneely. 1845.

Allegro.

829.

Fine.

D. C. al Segno.

Young lads that are prepared for marriage.

830.

208

One night I dreamt‡
also called "Are you not the bright star that used to be before me?"

‡ *Note*. Petrie adds "or Sweet Castle Hyde" in pencil.
* *Note*. Another version has no "repeat" marked here.
Another setting of this tune appears with Gaelic title Ed.

"Each night when I slumber."   From Mr. Joyce.

832.

Oh agus oh! oh! The blind woman's lament for the loss of her daughter.

833.

Ballyhauness.

834.

Slieve Gullan or The enchantment of Fin Mac Cool.   An Ossianic air.

835.

209

O'er high, high hills and lofty mountains.

836.

I'm an Irishman from Monaghan--a North country man born.

837.

Castle Costello.

838.

Note. The key signature should probably be two sharps. Ed.

A Munster tune:

839.

210

Assist me all ye muses. A county of Londonderry air.

840.

O sad and sorry I'm this day. A Derry Song.

841.

Garvagh! its a pretty place, surrounded well with trees.

842.

Rody green. A Co of Kilkenny air.

843.

Chorus.

Early in the morning – a county of Cavan air.

844.

You nobles of Inis Ealga.

845.

Art Mac Bride – a county of Donegal air.

846.

Harvest.⁺

847.

⁺Doubtful name, written very illegibly. Ed.

Mount Hazel.

848.

All the ways to Galway.

849.

The frost is all over. Set in the Co. of Armagh.

850.

She hung her Petticoat out to dry.

851.

Da Capo.

The highly excellent good man of Tipperoughny.   Co of Kilkenny. Revd Mr Graves.

852.

Note. These variants are given under the heading "The men of Tipperoughny." from Mr Fogarty. Ed.

An Iverk Love song (wants the 4th of the scale.) From the Revd Mr Graves.

853.

Be wise - beware! From J. Tighe Junior.

854.

The new broom.

855.

The new broom. From P. Conneely.

856.

Note. A variant of the preceding Ed.

214

Who'll buy my besoms.

Allegretto.

857.

2nd setting.

Allegretto.

858.

Dunlavin Green.

Set in the county of Wicklow.

859.

Flower of young maidens.

Moderato.

860.

Take a kiss or let it alone.

From Mr Pigot's M.S.

861.

Set by Mr Joyce in the Co of Limerick in 1856.   from the singing of Dd Condon.

862.

Note. Petrie adds: "This is the same air as Bunting's. When to a foreign clime I go."

When first I left old Ireland.   From a Mason in Belfast. P. McD.

Andante.

863.

Caoine

+Another version has E♭ in these places. Ed.

My blessing go with you sweet Erin go bragh.   From Mr Mac Dowell. Decr 1859.

Andante

864.

Note. Another version has E♮ here. Ed.

216

Emigrant song (going to America).

Andante quasi Allegretto.

865.

Old North American Indian tune.   From—Joly Esq. March 1860.

866.

Paddys return.

867.

Paddys evermore. Second set.

868.

Note. The M. S. has neither clef nor signature. **Ed.**

Five men went together.

869.

Five men went together
Five men went together
Four men, three men
Two men, one man
And the mower went to mow the meadow.

Mother ru a ru a ru a
Mother ru a rendy
With a stick upon her back
And another in her hand
Saying Good morrow to you kindly madam.

Note. Petrie adds a memorandum "Don't forget Molly Brollaghan."
The M S. has neither clef nor signature, and is very illegible. Ed.

Dancing measure to which Prince Charles Edward and Lady Wemyss danced in the
gallery of the palace of Holyrood House in the year 1745.   From Lord Rosmore.

870.

Planxty by Carolan, preserved in Clare.

Allegro moderato.
From Frank Keane 21. July 1858.

871.

Note. The accidentals in brackets are supplied from a second version of this tune, which occurs with a
signature of 2 flats Ed.

218

Dance tune or Planxty, apparently by Carolan.

From Mr. Mac Dowell March '59.

Allegro moderato.

872.

Note. This tune appears again under the title: "Do what you please but take care of my cup." The variants are indicated above. Ed.

Planxty Wilkinson by Carolan.

Allegro moderato.

873.

Note. The accidentals in brackets are supplied from another version. This tune also appears with the title "Planxty Williamson." Ed.

Planxty Drew by Carolan.

From P. Carew's MSS.

874.

Note. The accidentals in brackets are supplied from another version. Ed.

Planxty - by Carolan - set in Munster.   From Mr Kelly.

875.

Lady Wrixon.

876.

Note. Published in Petrie's "Ancient music of Ireland" as a planxty by Carolan. For a seventh planxty by
Carolan See No 499. Ed.

Planxty Sweeny.   From M. S. Mrs Close.

877.

220

Planxty Shane ruadh.   From Miss Simmonds.

Allegretto

878.

‡ The Hunt – a set Dance. From John Dolan – Glensheen.   Mʳ Joyce.

879.

‡ Also known as "The Galtee hunt." Ed.

"The Ladies fancy," or "The piper's finish." or the Long Dance.   Mʳˢ Close.

880.

Gather up the money — the Petticotee dance and song tune. R. M.✛

881.

✛ Richard Morrison, Esq.

Lower Ormond. A Dance tune.

882.

Long Dance.

883.

The Bruisus, or "Kiss the maid behind the barrels."

From Col. Westenra.

884. Allegro.

Kiss the maid behind the barrel. A Cork Reel.

From P. Carew's MSS.

885.

Note. A variant of the preceding. Ed.

Kiss the maid behind the barrel.

From F. Keane.

886. Allegro.

Note. A different version. Ed.

D.C.

Reel. Set in the county of Limerick. From Mrs. McSweeny.

From Mr. P. Joyce.

887. Allegro.

Note. Petrie adds "Kiss the maid etc." Cf. with the three preceding tunes. Ed.

Box about the fire place. A Munster Reel.

From P. Carew's MSS.

888.

Note. The variant accidentals are from a second version of this tune. Ed.

Last night's funeral - A Munster Reel.

From P. Carew's MSS.

889.

Munster Reel.

From Mr. P. Joyce.

890.

Boil the breakfast early - A Munster Reel.

From Mr. P. Joyce.

891.

"The job of journey work." A Munster Dance.   From Mr Joyce.

892.

The Peeler's jacket. A Munster Reel.   From Mr Joyce.

893.

Note. Petrie adds in pencil "Same as Flannel jacket."
See Nº 584. Ed.

+ Munster Reel.   From Mr Joyce.

894.

+ Petrie has a note in pencil "not to be used, too Scotch." Ed.

The Morning star. A Cork Reel.   From P. Carew's M.S.S.

895.

Note. Petrie adds "perhaps Scotch." Ed.

Munster Reel.

From P. Joyce.

Blackwater foot.

A Munster Reel.

The Goroum. A Reel.

From P. Carew's MS.

The Kerry star. A Reel.

From P. Carew's MS.

228

The bragging man. A Cork Reel.

From P. Carew's MSS.

Temple Hill. A Cork Reel.

From P. Carew's MSS.

Molly on the shore. A Cork Reel.
Allegro.

From P. Carew's MSS.

A Cork Reel.

From P. Carew's MSS.

903.

Allegro.

Fine.

D.C.

+ Another version gives this bar thus:

+ Another version gives this bar thus:

The new domain. A Cork Reel.

From P. Carew's MSS.

904.

A Clare Reel.

Frank Keane. From his Father. Mar. 10. 1856.

905.

Allegro.

County of Clare Reel.

From Frank Keane. Mar. 10. 1856.

906.

Allegro.

230

County of Clare Reel.   From Frank Keane.

907.

D.C.

County of Clare Reel.   From Frank Keane.

908.

Note. Petrie has probably omitted a one-sharp signature and consequently accidentals also. Ed

The green fields of Ireland.   A Connaught Reel.

909.

The country girl's fortune.

A Connemara Reel.

910.

D.C.

Lough Allen. An old county of Leitrim Reel.

911.

The gooseberry blossom.

A Reel.

912.

The silver mines. A Reel.

From Mr Joyce.

913.

Reel set from John Hickey. Ballyorgan.

From M? P. Joyce.

914.

Note. Petrie has obviously omitted the signature of one sharp. Ed.

Reel - queer name?

915.

Note. As above. Ed.

Reel time, from an old M. S. music book.

From M? P. Joyce.

916. **Allegro.**

Reel.

From M? P. Joyce.

917.

Note. The accidentals in brackets are supplied from another version. Ed.

The Ewe with the crooked horn. A Cork reel.   From P. Carew's M.S.

918

+ Petrie adds "Hornpipe" in pencil.

From Mr P. Joyce.
Learnt from his father.

Hornpipe.

919.

Good night, good night, and joy be with you. A munster jig set   From Mr P. Joyce.
                                                   from J. Buckley.

920.

234

Cherish the ladies. A Munster Jig.

From Mʳˢ Close.

921.

The lovely lad. A Munster single Jig from Ned Goggin.

From Mʳ P. Joyce.

Allegro.

922.

÷) Another version has C♯ here. Ed.

Tea in the morning. A Munster Jig from J. Buckley.

From Mʳ P. Joyce.

923.

Down with the tithes. A Munster Jig.

From F. Keane.

924.

Strop the razor. A Munster Jig.

925.

"Barrack Hill." This kind of Jig is called in Munster a single jig. It had a peculiar kind of Dance.✦

926.

✦)Petrie's Note. He also adds "Same as a Scotch tune." Ed.

The Croosting Cap. A. Munster Jig. From Wm Sheady.

P. Joyce.

927.

Munster Jig.

From F. Keane.

928.

fp

tr

÷ *Note.* Another version has C♯ in these places. Ed.

Munster Jig as played by James Sheedy a celebrated Munster piper who died — very old — about 30 years ago✝

Mr Joyce.

929.

✝ Petrie's note. Ed.

Munster Jig.

From F. Keane. Sept. 10th '54.

930.

Munster Jig as played by James Sheedy. From Michael Dineen, Coolfree, a Farmer.

Mr Joyce.

931.

Munster Jig from J. Hickey. Ballyorgan, Co. of Limerick.

P. Joyce.

932.

+ *Note.* Petrie adds in pencil "Hush the cat from the bacon. P. Carew's M.S." See N° 946. Ed.

Munster Jig.

From Mr Joyce.

933.

The Munsterman's Jig.

From the Hon. Col. Westenra.

934

238

Kiss in the shelter. A Connaught Jigg.

935.

The ladies march to the ball-room. A Connaught Jigg.

936.

The lads on the mountain. A Connaught Jigg.

937.

The Bucks of Ahasnagh. A Connaught Jigg.

938.

Connaught Jig.

939.

The Geese in the Bog. A Clare Jig.

From F. Keane.

940.

The Humours of Milltown. A Clare Jig.

941.

Note. Petrie gives this as the same as "Chasing the hare down the hill". See N⁰ 413. Ed.

240

Old Clare Jig.   From Frank Keane

942.

Co. Clare Jig.   **Allegro.**

943.

Note. The variant notes and the accidentals in brackets are taken from two other versions of this tune. The version with the sharp seventh is in D major. Ed.

A Clare Jig.   From F. Keane.

944.

Note. This tune also appears with one ♯ in the signature and no accidentals in the tune. Ed.

The galloping young thing. A Cork Jig.

From P. Carew's MSS.

945.

Hush the cat from the bacon- a Cork Jig.

From P. Carew's MSS.

946.

Old Cork Jig.

From Mr Joyce.

947.

A Sligo Jig.

948.

242

Jig (very fine) set from D. Cleary. Kilfinane. Co of Limerick.

From Mr Joyce.

949.

Note. Petrie marks this: "The girl I love (see other setting not good)." See No 540. Ed.

Black Rock. A Mayo Jig.

From Denis H. Kelly Esq.
15. Mar. 1856.

950.

Note. Change on 1st bar (Petrie.)

The Galway Jig.

From Lord Rosmore.

951.

A county of Leitrim Jig.

952.

The three little drummers. A county of Leitrim Jig.

953.

Variant of Nº 110.
Note. This tune also occurs with an F♯ throughout. Ed.

The three little drummers.

From P. Carew's MSS.

Allegro.

954.

A variant of the preceding. Ed.

A Leitrim Jig.

955.

A variant of Nº 952. Ed.

Wink and she will follow you. A Kerry Jig.

From Father Walsh. MS.

956.

244

"The Housemaid." Jig.

957.

Round the world for sport. A single Jig, set from Edward Goggin. Glenosheen.   Mr. Joyce.

958.

The girl I love. Jig.

959.   Allegro.

From P. W. Joyce Esq.

Note. See Nº 540. Ed.

The good fellows. Jig.

960.

✠Another version has D♮ here.
Note. A Duplicate of this tune has the first four bars "repeated." Ed.

The Swaggering Jig.

From Mrs. Close.

The Bungalow Jig.

Allegro.

The Cauliflower Jig.

Allegro.

From P. Mac Dowell, Esq.

Jig from D. Cleary. Kilfinane.

From Mr. Joyce.

A second set of the above from James Buckley.

From M.ʳ Joyce.

965.

Jig or March.

From T. Davis.

966. Allegro.

Note. A variant of the preceding. Ed.

Jig.

From M.ʳ Joyce.

967. Allegro.

Jig.

From Col. Westenra.

968.

247

248

Jig.   From Mr. Joyce.

Allegro.

972.

+ *Note.* A second version of this tune has C♯ in these places. Ed.

Jig.   From Mr. Joyce.

(?A)

973.

Jig.   From F. Keane.

Allegro.

974.

Title has "Rory O' Moore" in pencil see N° 740 Ed.   *D. C.*

Jig.

975.

Jig.

976.

Note. Petrie calls this a jig to "General Wynne"(March tune Nº 986) Ed.

Jig.

977.

Allegro.

Time of day - a Hop jig - same melody as "Ride a mile".   From Mr. Joyce.

978.

2nd time

3rd time

250

A Hop Jig. County of Clare.

From F. Keane.

979.

Hop Jig.

980.

Allegro.

Carolan's favorite Jig.

981.

Ancient Munster March and Jig.

as set by Mr Joyce.

982.

Ancient Clan March.

983.

Ancient Clare March and Jig.

From Frank Keane.

984.

Sir Patrick Bellew's March.

985.

252

General Wynne. A March by Carolan.

986.

Carlwac's March.

987.

"Favorite March of the old Irish Volunteers".

March Time.

From an old M.S. Music Book.

988.

The Irish Lad's a jolly boy. A favourite march of the old Irish militia bands.

989.

A slight variant of N⁰ 586.
Cf. "The Breeches on" N⁰ 473 Ed.

253

The Hurlers' march.

990.

First time.   Second time.

First time.   Second time.

Ree Raw, or The Butchers' March.

991.

Carpenter's March.

992.

Chorus.

The Ribbonman's march, set by W. Forde.   From Mr. Pigot's M.S.

993.

Oh woman of the house, isn't that neat?

994.

Note The title is given in Petrie's index as: "O woman of the house is not that pleasant? A white - boy march." Ed.

Joy be with you - an ancient Connaught March for "breaking up."

995.

Vive la! the French are coming.   A Rebel March song.

March Time.

996.

The Buachalin og March.

From Frank Keane.

997.

"The Housekeeper," A March.

From M.r Joyce.

998.

Dance or Quick March.

From M.r R. A. Fitzgerald.

Allegro.

999.

March and Jig.

M.rs Close.

1000.

D.C.

A March tune.

1001.

256

Ancient Lullaby.

From F. Keane 1st October. 1854

Andantino.

1002.

Clare Lullaby.

From Frank Keane - Oct. 1st 1854.

Andantino.

1003.

or thus:

hush o!

Sligo Lullaby.

From Mr. Owen O'Conellan. 13. December. 1858.

1004.

A Lullaby.

Got by Forde from Mr. O'Brien, Cork.

Andante.

1005.

mf   cresc.   p   ppp

A Lullaby.

Andante.

1006.

hush o.

Note. This is the same tune as *№* 83 with slight differences of rhythm in the repeated bars. Ed.

A Lullaby.

From Miss Ross.

1007.

p   pp   ppp

A Lullaby.

Mr. Joyce from Davy Condon. Ballyorgan. C? of Limerick.

Lullaby or Nursery song.

From T. Bridgeford.

Nurse's tune or. Hushaby.
Andante.

From P. Coneely.

Nurse Tune.

From Mr. Joyce.

Nursery song.

From James O' Reilly Esq.

Hush a by baby on the tree top,
When the wind blows the cradle will rock.
When the bough bends the cradle will fall,
Down comes the baby, cradle and all.

Nursery song.   From Walter Sweetman Esq

1013.

Nurse tune.   From J. Mac Mahon.

1014.   Andante.

The Fairy Nurse's song — an air of the county.   Farney — Co. of Monaghan.

1015.

Cradle song (Hush oh my Lanna), as sung by T. Bridgeford.

1016.

Hush oh my Lanna Hush oh my Lanna Hush oh my Lanna my Lanna ma chree.

Cradle Hymn.   From Mr. Southwell.

1017.   Andante.

The Dirge of Ossian - as sung in the glens in Derry.

1018.

The Lamentation of Deirdre for the sons of Usnach. Set in Mayo.

1019.

Lament for Una Mac Dermot.

1020.

Note. This air also appears under the title "Caoine for Winifred McDermot, Roscommon." Ed.

Donald Baccagh's lament. A county of Derry air.

1021.

Carolan's lamentation for Charles Mac Cabe. "Parting from a companion." Forde.

Andante.

1022.

Wood's lamentation.

by Carolan.

1023.

(Lucuna.)

Soggarth Shamus O'Finn. A lament.

Moderato.

1024.

+ *Note.* Another version has C ♮ in these two places. Ed.

The Lamentation of Sir Richard Cantillon.

Madden.

1025.

The lament of William Mc Peter the outlaw.

1026.

+Petrie has a pencil note here.- "Mem. To correct this phrase, which should be in 4 bars". Ed.

In Horncastle's work called "Ormonde's Lament."

From old M.S. of Mrs. Close.

1027.

The Phillelew

262

The Hare's lament.

1028.

The Lament as sung in the Bennada glens.   Co of Londonderry.

1029.

*Note.*The M.S. also has pencil bar lines beginning after the third quaver Ed.

A lament.

Andantino.

1030.

Keen.   from Mary Madden.

1031.

Ancient Caoine."Said to be the most ancient in the Provinces of Leinster and Munster."

Adagio.

1032.

Mr Joyce, from D. Condon.

A Caoine.

1033.

Caoine.

1034.

Caoine.

1035.

Caoine.

1036.

Caoine.

1037.

Note. A variant of the preceding. Ed.

264

The Plaint as sung in the parish of Bannagher.

1038.

Ancient Hymn tune, and Caoine.

1039.

Funeral cry.   Galway. August 28th 1840.

Agitato.

1040.

Irish cry.

1041.

Ancient Hymn.

Andantino.

1042.

Irish Hymn sung on the dedication of a chapel – Co. of Londonderry.

Note. Cf the opening phrase in the minor of "Soggarth Shamus O' Finn" No. 1024 Ed.

Ancient Hymn tune sung in country chapels. (An attempt to put it into rhythm.)

From Forde.

Another attempt to phrase this air.

Hymn tune.   Mr. Joyce, from his father.

Chant, or Hymn tune. Co. Donegal from Revd. James Mease, Freshford.

Andante.

266

The Hymn of St. Bernard. Jesu dulcis memoria.　　From Mr Southwell.

Andante.

1048.

Dies Irae — or Day of Wrath — as sung in the Co of Londonderry.

1049.

Christmas Carol or Hymn, — as sung in the county of Galway.　　From Mrs Close.

1050.

Plough whistle.

1051.

Note. The two B's in the 6.th bar and the 5 B's in the 10.th, 11.th, and 12.th bars are slurred in Petrie's "Ancient Music of Ireland." Ed.

T. Mac Mahon.

Ploughman's Whistle.

1052.

Plough song or whistle of the county of Kilkenny. ✦

From James Fogarty.

Slow.

1053.

✦ *Note.* Petrie's M.S. has no ♯ to this D, but in "Ancient Music of Ireland" he adds one. Ed.

T. Mac Mahon.

Ploughman's Whistle.

1054.

Plough song.

From Mac Mahon.

1055.

Welcome home Prince Charley.

1056.

⁺ *Note*. The above fragment occurs, written in pencil, without clef or signature in Petrie's manuscript
He adds the following note: "Where were you all day, - another so called Scots air, - is the Irish Sean a cacan
or John of the quill" See "Where were you all the day, my own pretty boy." N° 330 Ed.

When she answered me her voice was low.

1057.

⁺ *Note*. See the more usual form of this tune in three-bar phrase, N° 251 and 613 Ed.

1058.

⁺ *Note*. The above tune is without name and is made up from two almost illegible pencil jottings in Petrie's M S S.
Ed.

1059.

⁺ *Note*. Compare with N° 898 and 899. Ed.

The Petrie Collection of Irish Music.

PART III

Set in the county of Derry.

1060.

Ceaṅ ɒuḃ ɒíliɼ.

Set in county of Londonderry.

1061.

Ceaṅ ɒuḃ ɒíliɼ.

Set in the county of Derry.

Allegretto.

1062.

bímiɒ aʒ ól'ɼ aʒ póʒaɒ na mban.

From Father Walsh.

Let's be drinking.

1063.

bímío aʒ ól 'ʃa póʒaó na mban.

From T. Mac Mahon

1064.

CHORUS.

"Ppíeʃc", a ṁopnín!

1065.

The melody of the Harp.

Ceólʒa Cpuiʒ.

1066.

Moreen.

Dóipín.

From O' Neill's collection A. D. **1787.**

1067.

+*Note.* The original version of Moore's "Minstrel Boy." Ed.

Nóirín bán.

From Mrs. Close.

1068.

Dóirín na trí bainne, nó abrán ní Raigallaig.

1069.

The strolling mason.

An rábuire raoir.

From Mary Madden.

1070.

Andante.

A second set of the above air.

An rábuire raor.

From Frank Keane.

1071.

Andante.

272

1 Miltown a ċuala mé an ceól.

In Miltown I heard the music.

Set from Margaret Hickey.

1072.

1 Milltown a ċuala mé an ceól.

2nd setting of preceding.

Set from Bridget Monahan.

1073.

bríġio inġen Ṡuiḃne ḃán.

1074.

Daiġdean aɜ ɾɜaɾaḋ lé na ɜráḋ.

The Maiden's lament for her lover's departure.

Skull. P. Mc Dowell.

Andante.

1075.

Aip maidin i noé.

Yesterday morning, and I about to sleep.

Set from T. Mac Mahon 1857.

A Song ✠ between William English and Shane Claragh's wife.

Andante.

1076.

✠ *Note.* This word is uncertain. The binder of the Petrie MSS. has cut it in two Ed.

Do čailín don veaṛ a'ṛ miṛe aṛ ól.

Mr Joyce from Davy Condon.

Andante.

1077.

Do ṛiúbal me Éiṛe ó'n ṛcúan ṛo céile.

From T. Mac Mahon.

1078.

✠ *Note.* A variant of the preceding. Ed.

Úaiṛ beṛ ṛoiṁ an lá.

From O' Neill's collection.

Slow and with solemnity. (♮)

1079.

✠ *Note.* The accidentals in brackets are supplied from another version of this Tune. Ed.

274

Úaıɾ ƀẽᵹ ɾoıṁ an lá.

A little hour before day.

1080.

Note. A variant of the preceding. Ed. ✛ Another version has G♯ in these places. Ed.

baınıɾ Śeáın.

1081.   **Andante.**

Ráca bɾeáᵹ mo ċın.

The pretty hair comb. From Skull. Co. of Cork. P. Mac Dowell Esq.

1082.

Daɾéᵭ nıᵹ Ɗuƀaɾtaḃ.

From Frank Keane.

1083.   **Allegretto.**

✛ *Note.* Another version has E♭ in these places. Ed.

Pír fliuč.

From P. Carew's MS.

1084.

Táinig an Wata am' Látair gan moill.

From Frank Keane.

Andante.

1085.

'Sé an baile feo togaò na oroč áite.

From Frank Keane.

1086.

A òrioċáir ir oiombáò tú luaò lé mnaoi.

1087.

A béan a' tíġe na páirte.

Andante.

1088.

Saġairt tar teórad.

1089.

Do rtóirín ó Ḋurċaiḋe.

Mʳ Joyce from L. O'Brien.

1090.

Who could see noble Cormac.   Cé t'iḋread Cormac uaṛal.   From Teige Mac Mahon.

Allegretto.

1091.

baint ḟrníḋe ṛaoi ḃuillġḃaṛ na ġcraoḃ.   Mʳ Joyce from L. O'Brien.

1092.

✝ Another version has a♭ in these places. Ed.

Cipig aip maroin ir ʒaib oo capall ir bailiʒ leat má ḟéoaip.

From Frank Keane.

Allegretto.

1093.

Aʒ an mbaile núaó a tá an bḟpuinʒeall móoaṁail mná.

From Mʳ Joyce.

Allegretto.

1094.

Do ʒráó bán am' tpeiʒean a'p céile oá luaó leir.

Mʳ Joyce, from Lewis O'Brien.

Andante.

1095.

Coppaió oo ćopa a Śeáinín.

Mʳ Joyce, from Ned Goggin.

Allegro.

1096.

Ir í mo leanb (Caoine).

From Mr Joyce.

1097.

Cailín ruad gaedealac.

The Irish lass with the golden tresses. A Sligo tune.

1098.

Petrie's Note: - This tune was obtained by me from an old gentleman in the year 1810, who was then about 93 years of age, - Owen Connellan, Professor of Celtic Languages, Queen's College, Cork. His mother, from whom he got it died aged 110. See Nº 46 which is evidently Petrie's original jotting for this Tune. Ed.

An Cailín ruad.

1099.

An Cailín ruaḋ.

From O'Neill's collection.

1100.

An Cailín ruaḋ.

From P. Joyce Esq.

1101.

Feaḋ ġiolla na reirríġe aġur na cairte.

The ploughboy and cart boy's whistle.

From T. Mac Mahon.

1102.

Note. For other plough-whistles see № 1051 to 1055. Ed.

Dá mbéiḋeḋ mo ġráḋ-ṡa 4 láṛ ḋo ċroíḋe-ṛe.

Mary Madden.

If my love were within your heart.

1103.

A Kerry air, also called "The true love knot." Petrie's note. Ed.

Dúirṗín ġeal mo ċroíḋe.

1104.

Cappaiġín an Fáṫaċ.

A Mayo air.

1105.

Note. See "A woman and twenty of them" Nọ 816 Ed.

Well, laoġ mo ċroíḋe.

1106.

An Púca.

A Connemara tune.

1107.

Dóp inġean Taiḋġ óiġ.

1108.

Caıtleaċa ó ṫuaıḋ.

The Northern Hags. A Connaught jig.

1109.

Clıbeaᵹ ḃaıle an ḃoṫeıᵹ; Mackey ḃaıle an ṫléıḃe.

1110.

*Note. This title is given by Petrie in English characters thus "Clibig volin vorey nackey walan Slava." Ed.

Iṫ ṫuaᵹ mé, ᵹan mo ᵹṫáḋ.

1111.

A ṫaıḃ ṫú aᵹ an ᵹcaṫṫaıᵹ?

1112.

Péaṙla ḋeaṙ ón ṫṙliaḃ ḃán.

From O'Neill's collection. 1787

1113.

Note. See "The Roving Pedlar," Nº 360. Ed.

Péaṙla ḋeaṙ an ṫṙléiḃ ḃáin.

The beautiful pearl of Slieve Bán.

1114.

Note. A variant of the preceding. Ed.

beaṅ an ḟiṙ ṙuaiḋ.

Allegro.

From Lord Rosmore.

1115.

Aip maroin a-noé, bí camaoain rzoil.

A. Munster tune.

1116.

21 téżaip an piop buit naċ żcobluiżim-re oíoċe.

Knowest thou my dear that I sleep not at night.

1117.

bpírte bpéioín.

A Hop jig.   From Lord Rosmore.

1118.

Uam Ríoż.

The King's Cave. An Arran boat-song.   From Lord Rosmore. Set in 1841.

In rowing time.

1119.

Cuppaig Diapmuid do'n capall beg.

A Jig.

1120.

Séid, a bean boict! 7 bí rúgać.

Blow old woman and be merry.

From P. W. Joyce.

1121.

Nóra an Čoirc.

1122.

Easter snow, or, properly, +Direapt Huadain; nó Sneačta Cárga.

P. W. Joyce. 1864

1123.

+The name of a place in the C? of Mayo. Petrie's Note. Ed.

Ceir Corran.

From P. W. Joyce.

1124.

"A mountain in C? Sligo." Petrie's note Ed.

Síor 1 mears na scoillte.

Down among the woods. A Mayo tune.

P.W. Joyce. March 1864.

Andante.

1125.

An cailín a tá 1 n-aice Shligig.

The girl who is near Sligo.   March 1864. A C? Mayo tune.

1126.

A Dáire! 'r a múirnín!

From the Revd. J. Goodman.
Ardgroven, Castletown Bere.
Dec. 3rd 1863.

O Mary my darling.

Plaintive.

1127.

Tá mé rápuiġ; b'ḟeápp liom 'ran mbaile.

The Prodigal Son. Now I am tired and wish I was at home.

Set by Forde.

Andante.

1136.

Ir cailín beż óż mé.

"I'm a young little girl."

From Mary O' Malley Arran More Sept. 7th 1857.

Andante.

1137.

bean ouḃ an ġleaña.

Andante.

1138.

Oómnall mo ṁian.

Donnell my Love.

From Mr. Mac Dowell. March 1859.

Andante.

1139.

bean an fir ruaḋ.

As sung by Mary Madden.

1140.

Andante.

"Saḋon" na réḋ.

Mr. Joyce.
From Joseph Martin. Kilfinane.

1141.

Moderato.

Ḋala an Tyḣo!

Called also "A new broom sweeps clean" and "Sweet Innismore".

From F. Keane.

1142.

Andante.

Note. A variant of this tune may be found under its English title "Sweet Innismore"., Nº 376. Ed.

Ḋia ḃeaċa do ḟláinte; a ḟár-ḟir ċóir!
Cuirim ʒo lá céo míle ḟáilte róṁac.

From F. Keane.

1143.

Moderato.

Aṗẓúp an ḃaile peo.

Arthur of this town.

Allegretto.

From Mr. O. O'Conellan.

1144.

Fa ḟpaoċ na coillġċ bpice.

Andante.

From Mr. Owen O'Conellan.

1145.

An cuiṁin leaẓ aṅ ṅn, ḃíoṁap aɜ ḟiaċaċ ḟáʼn nɜleaṅ.

Do you remember the time we were hunting in the valley.

Andante.

From Mr. Owen O'Conellan.

1146.

Ẓap liom ḍoʼn aonaiɜ.

Come with me to the fair.

Allegro moderato.

From Mr. Owen O'Conellan.

1147.

Dómna� ó bṗíaın.

From F. Keane Nov.ʳ 28. 58.

1148.

Petrie adds "This seems to be a tune of Carolan's." Ed

I never will deceive you, ᴀ Sᴄóᴩ ᴍo ċᴩoíᴆe!

I never will deceive you.

Andante

1149.

Δóᴩ. ní ḃᴇ5: nó Ċ'óᴍoň ā ċnoıc.

1150.

✝) Sic. Ed.

5ıᴌe ḃᴇ5 ᴌé ᴍ'ᴀnᴀᴍ ᴄú.

From F. Keane 19ᵗʰ July. 58.

1151.

✝) or thus:

292

Abaiṁ, a Cumain, ḟil!

Andante.

1152.

 Na ġaṁna ġeala bána.

Lively.

1153.

Na ġaṁna ġeala bána.

Allegro.

1154.

Note. A Variant of the preceding. Ed.
Note. Petrie gives the signature of two sharps. The tune is still known as above. Ed.

An ġaḃan ġeal bán.

Set from J. Buckley.   Mr Joyce.

Allegretto.

1155.

Sṁáḋ mo ċléiḃ.

Andante.

Set from L. O! Brien. Mr. Joyce.

1156.

bé Eireaṅ í.

Slow.

From the Rev. James Goodman.

1157.

bé n Eiriṅ í.

Andante.

Set from J. Martin. Mr. Joyce.

1158.

Ceó ḋruíḋeaċta.

From Mr. Joyce. p. 23.

1159.

A Ċuıṙle ġeal mo ċṙoíḋe.

From Mr. Joyce.

1160.

Do ġráḋ! mo ċeaṙc!

A woman's lament for the death of her Hen. From P. Mac Dowell Esq.

Andantino.

1161.

Óṙán an uıġ.

From Mr. Joyce. p. 71.

1162.

Ḋáıṙe ḃeaṙ.

Andante.

From P. Mac Dowell Esq.

1163.

An cnoicín fraoíg.

Andante.

Set from J. Buckley. From Mr. Joyce.

1164.

Iṫ aiṙ maiḋin ḋom ḋia lúain.

From Miss Williams, heard at Kilmallock.

1165.

Iṫ aiṙ maiḋin ḋom ḋia lúain.

From P. Carew's MSS

1166.

Note. A slight variant of the preceding.

Coiṙ na briġḋe.

as set by Dr. Hudson at Clonakilty — and given to Forde.

Andante.

1167.

Petrie adds note "This air, which is fine, seems obviously to be a form of the "Clar bug deal" with the..... transposed" (Part of his note has been cut off by the binder) See following tune. Ed.

An clár bog "déil",

Grave.

or "Cashel of Munster."

1168.

Note. A variant of "The soft deal board." See Nos 581 and 582. Ed.

Coir na bríżoe.

pia

1169.

Note. A variant of the preceding.

Dáire an čúil fiń.

Andante.

From P. Coneely.

1170

Dallí bán.

Andante.

From F. Keane.

1171.

298

Caoine—do cuaid mé, ár tu-ra.

With tremulous expression of feeling.   From F. Keane.

1176.

Óc ón! a cuid an traoigil.

Andante.   Mayo air.
                                                         From Dr. Kelly.

1177.

Ir truag mé! i Saranaig.

Andante.   From Mr. Pigot's M.S.

1178.

or

Ir truag mé! i Saranaig.

Andante.

1179.

The same air as the preceding. Different set. Petrie's note. Ed.

Róir geal dub.

Andante.   From Tuam. P. Mac Dowell Esq.

1180.

Note. The variants are taken from a second version of this tune. Ed.

An coṁleaċ ġlaṙ an ḟóġṁaiṙ.

"On the green stubble of Autumn."
From Mary Madden 9ᵗʰ Dec. 55.

1181.

An t-ṙean ḃean ċaiṫṙaċ.

From Mr. Hardiman's M.S.

1182.

Iṙ ṙeal úꝺ ꝺoṁ aṙ ḃṙiaṙaiḃ.

Andante.

From Mr. Hardiman's M.S.

1183.

Cúl na muice.

Allegretto.

From Mr. Hardiman's M.S.

1184.

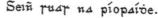

Do bṗón ṡan miṡe'ṡan ṡṗéiṡ-ṡéan!

1195.

báṡ an uiṡṡe ḃeaṡá.

Sung in the Bannagher glens. Derry.

1196.

Róṡa ḃṡeaṡṡaṡ.

Sung in the Bennada glens, Cọ of Derry.

1197.

Haṡ miṡe an ceaṅ cinṡiṡ.

A Mayo air.

1198.

Note. Petrie writes this Gaelic title in English characters thus:- "Nogh mise un cian einrich? Ed.

Tá mo ṡṡáṗ aiṡ ḃaṡ na ṡméṡa.

As sung in the Bennada glens. Derry.

1199.

304

Scíat Lúiṙeaċ Ḋuiṙe.

An ancient Hymn. Also the melody of Ossian's poem of Tale.

The Cuckoo's nest.   An ṙealadóiṙ.

bean a ṫaḃaiṙne.   Or, the Hostess.

An paláiṙin muiṁneaċ.

An Palaingin Muineac.

1209.

Cremóna.

Carolan.

1210.

Note. The title is in English characters thus: "Cremonea" Ed.

Táillúp an éadaig.

or, The taylor of the cloth.

Gaily.

1211.

Fan map táip, a Clavóipe!

A Munster jigg.

1212.

Ó! mo ċailín; d'imṫiġ rí!

As sung by a little girl heard at the foot of Slieve Gullan in 1807.

J. Tighe.

1213.

Ó! mo ċailín, d'imṫiġ rí!

Allegretto.

1214.

Note. A variant of the preceding. Ed.

Cia in bealaċ a nḋeaċaiġ rí?

1215.

Cé'n bealaċ a nḋeaċaiġ rí?

"Which way did she go."

1216.

CHORUS.

Note. A variant of the preceding. Ed.

Briġid an ċúil ḃáin.

Or, Brigid of the fair hair. A Munster air, set in Caher.

Moderately.

1217.

Da Capo.

An caitín voñ.

1218.

Caoíne na ʀean-aoíʀe.

Oʀ "the lament of old age." County Clare Tune.

1219.

CHORUS.

Ní ólʀiò mé ní aʀ mó eiʀ na bóż'ʀaiǧ ʀeo Šliǧiǧ.

A Sligo Melody.

1220.

Ní ólʀiò mé ní aʀ mó aʀ na bóżʀe ʀeo Šliǧiǧ.

1221.

Note. A slight variant of the preceding. Ed.

Ní óiℓṙió mé ní aℓ mó aiℓ na bóṫ'ℓaiʒ ℓeo Šℓiʒiʒ.

1222.

Note. Petrie places a signature of B flat and A flat at the beginning of this tune. Ed.

Seáʒan ʒaḃa.

An Erris Melody.

1223.

Seán ʒaḃa.

An Erris Melody.

1224.

Note. A variant of the preceding. Ed.

Seanṁuine cam.

Or,"the young wife and the old man," as sung in the county of Mayo.

1225.

SHE

HE

Note. The following 3 bars   appear in pencil above the ending in Petrie's MSS. (He had originally written the second part of the tune throughout in 9/8.)He also adds: "Transpose this into D minor two notes higher)." See Nọ 529 Ed.

Seán buíðe.

1226.

A múipnín! ɼláinte!

1227.

✠ Sic in M.S.Ed.

buaċaillín buíðe.

1228.

Uıl-le-hú! mo ṁáilín.

From T. Mac Mahon.

1229.

CHORUS.

Note. Petrie adds "See Mr.Joyce's set of this air." Ed.

Uih-hú! mo ṁáilín.

1230.

An cúircín láṅ.

From Father Walsh.

1231.

An cúircín láṅ.

Lively.

Kerry version.

1232.

Iṡ maiṫ an ouine ṫú.

Andante.

From Miss Williams, heard at Askeaton.

1233.

Is maiṫ an ouine ṫú.

Very Slow.   Scorching is this love.   From Father Walsh.

1234.

1235.

1236.

1237.

✦These ornaments appear in a different form in Petrie's printed Collection Ed.

An ᴅᴘeóillín (The Wren).

Caillᵉaċ a ṁapḃuiżiᴘ mé.

"Hag, you've killed me."   From Father Walsh.

Aiᴘ Éiᴘe, ní (i)ñeóᴘaiñ ciaḣí.

For Eire I'd not tell her name.

An ʒaṙún óʒ a ċṙáḋaiʒ mé.

County of Limerick. From P. Mac D.

1238.

An ʒaṙún óʒ ḋo ċṙáḋaiʒ mé.

1239.

Note. A very slight variant of the preceding. Ed.

Róiṗín ḋuḃ.

C? of Cork air. Mr. Watson.

1240.

Note. Petrie gives the signature of two sharps. There should probably be but one. Ed.

Róiṗín ḋuḃ.

1241.

Is fad ó geall tú éilim liom.

"'Tis long ago you promised to steal away with me."

P. Conneely.

Scilléd dub.

Andante.

1243.

Scilléd dub.

1244.

Note. A variant of the preceding. Ed.

Scilléd dub.

1245.

Note. Another variant of Nº 1243. Ed.

Is gorta čugut-ṡa.

1246.

÷ ? Ed.

Saṁaiṗc ċaṗ ceóṗaḃ.

from the Chief Baron. Jan. 1. 1852.

1247.

Petrie adds note, "As I doubt if this should not be in 6/8 time, do not copy it." Ed.

Ouḃ nú bán.

"Are you not the bright star that used to be before me?"

1248.

Note. A variant of N° 831. Ed.

A ḃean a' ciġe na ṗáiṗce.

1249.

Sluġup an ṁeaḋaiṗ.

Or, The gurgling of the churn.

1250.

ff

Coir na briġde.

Maestoso dolce.

1251.

p

ad lib.   dolce   cresc.

p

Note. This air is not in Petrie's handwriting. Ed.

Tá mé i mo ċoḋlaḋ.

From Mr. J. Keane's book, Kilrush.

1252.

Tá mé (aġ) cleamnaſ.

"The banks of the daisies."

Ealying song. W. Ford.

1253.

A ḃuaċaillíḋe! Cúnġnaiġe lé ċéile: nó
An ḃuaċaillín ḋonn.

Oh Boys help each other.

Croppy song. F. Keane.

1254.

Note. "The true name of this air appears to be the Buacailin donn. It has been set by Mr. Joyce from the single (singing?) of Mary Hackett, a native of Limerick, now in Dublin." (Petrie.) This tune is known also as "The Maid of Cooley Shore." Ed.

316

An buaċaillín voṅ, nó Cúaille in plé-náca.

From Teige Mac Mahon.

1255.

buaċaillín voṅ.

1256.

Note. The small notes in the last few bars are in pencil in Petrie's handwriting For a variant of this tune see "Never despise an old friend." No 675. Ed.

+ An buaċaill ban.

From O'Neill's MS. Vol. 1787.

1257.

Note. The title has a pencil note (not in Petrie's hand) "Same as night closed around the conqueror's way."
Ed.

búaċallán buíóe.*

A Munster jigg.

1258.

Note. This tune also appears in 6/8 time. The accidentals are supplied from a second version in A major.
*Written by Petrie "Bruithe" as in No 96.

An buačaillín buiðe.

From J. Keane.

1259.

An búačaill caol ꝺub.

1260.

An búačaill caol ꝺub.

From Paddy Conneely.

1261.

Note. A variant of the preceding. Ed.

An búačaill caol ꝺub.

1262.

Note: A variant of Nº 1261. Ed.

318

Ir buaċaillín óg mé, gan ór, gan ċuid.

I am a young boy, without gold or stock"

Kate Kane.

1263.

An Rógaire voill.

From J. Mac Mahon.

1264.

Note. See the variant of this (in the minor) called "Oh my love she was born in the North Country wide." No. 516. Ed.

An "Rógaire vub.

Or the black rogue. A. Munster jigg, formed on the air "Brigid of the fair hair." *

1265.

* See No. 1217 Ed.

buaċaillín óg.

From the Carew MSS.

1266.

Note. This tune also appears with no sharp in the signature. Ed.

Ʒaineaḃ buíḋe.

The yellow sands.

Sung in the Bannagher glens.

1267.

Ʒainem buíḋe.

A Song of the Bannagher glens.

1268.

Note. A rhythmical variant of the preceding. Ed.

Cairíoɣeċ bán; nó buaċaill caol ouḃ.

County of Mayo tune.

1269.

Note. A variant of Nº 1261. Ed.

320

Seán a búrca (John de Burgo, or Burke).

1270.

Seán a búrca.

1271.

Note. A variant of the preceding. Ed.

An ancient Clan march.

búrcap.

1272.

Note. The variants are taken from a second version which is otherwise identical with this. Ed.

Gráó geal mo cpoíóe.

Set at the Fair of Slane. Sept. 3rd 1842.

1273.

1274.

Note. A slight variant of the preceding. Ed.

buaċaillín áġbéil.

The stout little Boy.   From Frank Keane.

1275. Andante.

1276. ?

Note. This tune appears several times, always with an undecipherable Gaelic title written phonetically in English characters thus: "Ninny Vorha." Ed.

Tá mé i mo ċoḋlaḋ 'r ná ḋúiriġ mé.   Set in Arran More.

1277.

1278. Allegretto. ?

Note. This tune occurs twice with an undecipherable Gaelic title, written phonetically in English characters thus: Woley farthach na witlah cratah fanhil patraie trugh go lure. Ed. (Cf. The Finale of Berlioz's Faust.)

322

1279.

Iſ ʒan áıꝛo mé ʒan mátaıꝛ.

Andante.   (♮)   From F. Keane.

1280.

Note. The accidentals in brackets are supplied from another version of this tune. Ed.

1281.

1282.

Flano óg, p.

1283.

Petrie adds note "Should have been set in F." Ed . The Phonetic English title of this is written as follows :— "Fland og choine sdas muinter agus the dire." Ed.

Suzpa na zcapa . . . . +

1284.

Note. The Gaelic title of this air appears written in phonetic English characters thus :— "Sugra na garah is a dharmagh la blean". Ed.

1285.

Note. A variant of the preceding. Ed.

Sung in the Benada glens.

1286.

A Leaċnapaiġ an . . . . +

Caoine.   Slow.

1287.

Cronan.

+)*Note.* The word omitted here is written "guish" in Petrie's MSS. Ed.

A 'Róg'-aire! stad!

1288.

A 'Róg'-aire! rtad!

1289.

Note. A variant of the preceding. Ed.

Gráó geal mo ċroíóe.

County of Cork. From P. Mac Dowell, Esq.

1290.

Ar ron blú oub an ġleaña.

1291.

Cé círeaḋ rúo murtaiġ.

1292. Allegro.

CHORUS.

or "The one horned cow."

bó, bó, bó na leat-aiḋirce!

from Mac Mahon.

1293.

Note: See Nos. 340, 341, 342. Ed.

báṗbaṗa níġ Ḋómnaill.

1294. Allegretto.

Óč! óč on! mo ḃrón a'r mo ṁilleaḋ.

An ancient Munster air.

1295.

CHORUS.

tr

Óč! óč on! mo ḃrón a'r mo ṁilleaḋ.

1296.

tr

Note: A variant of the preceding. Ed.

326

Óṗán Caiṗleáin na hacéṁe.

1297.

Note. Castle Hackett, near Tuam.

Aḃṗán Caiṗleáin na hacéṁe.

1298.

An ċoṛ ṽeaṛ i mḃṛóṁ.

1299.

A coṛ ṽeaṛ i mḃṛóṁ.

1300.

Note: A variant of the preceding. Ed.

Ó ꝛa a ċumaiṅ ṁ ġil!

1301.

† Ġiní ċuġꝛaiṅ éluġuð leat.

Set in the County Derry.

1302.

Note. The Phonetic English title of this tune appears as follows: "Ginney Hugtuin chinliat." Ed.

Lá ḟéil' Páðꝛaic; no poċꝛéꝛeaċċ.

1303.

Suaꞃ lé m'ṁaiġðean ꞃuaꞃ an ꞃċaiꞃe.

Or "I went with my maiden up stairs."

From Mac Mahon, Co of Clare.

1304.

Racað-ꞃa ꝼá'n ꞃliaḃ; no i n-aiðaꞃca na ḃꝼiað.

Or "I will go to the mountain" or "to the Roebuck pinnacles."

From Mac Mahon.

1305.

328

Dúpnín na ṫpúaiṫe voñ-ḃuiḋé!

From Mac Mahon.

1306.

bpíṫio óṫ na ṫcumann.

Andante.

1307.

O young Bridget my beloved.   A bpíṫio óiṫ na ṫcumaṅ!

From T. Mac Mahon.

1308.

Note. A variant of the preceding. Ed.

Vá ḃṗáṫaiñ-ṙe an ṫ-ṙaiṫċuaċ.

From Teige Mac Mahon.

1309.

Píce an t-rúgra.

From Teige Mac Mahon.

1310.

A ṁaol! a tá mo ṁíle gráð leat.

O Mael, I am ruined by you.

From T. Mac Mahon.

1311.

An í an píṡ a tá uait? tá ṡí in ṡeo.

If it is the pea you want, it is here; called also
"The Bold Sportsman", and "The Carpenter's March".

1312.

Note: A variant of the preceding. For another tune, under the title "Carpenter's March" see No. 992 .Ed.

An rúiṡín buíðe.

The yellow blanket.

From the O'Neil MSS.

1313.

An ṙuiṙín báɴ.

The Shusseen ban.

1314.

(+? The signature of three flats omitted. Ed.

Lament.

Úɴa ṙúaṫ.

Andantino.

1315.

Caoíɴe.

From Kate Keane.

1316.

Note. A variant of Nº 1033. Ed.

Caoíɴe.

From Mary Madden.

Andantino.

1317.

Note. A variant of Nº 200 Ed.

An botar ó čuaið go Tpáž-lí.

The Northern road to Tralee. An ancient Clare March.

1318.

Note. This tune also appears (Nº 448) under its English title with some few differences of rhythm. Ed.

Fáȝfamoíð piúð map a tá pé.

1319.

Note. See Nº 387 Ed.

Caílín ðub.

Set in the County of Derry, 1834.

1320.

An caílín púað.

The "Caillin Ruadh."

1321.

332

Do Cailín ruaḋ.

From Mr. Joyce, b.b.p.62.

Andante.

1322.

An cailín ruaḋ.

1323.

An cailín ruaḋ.

The Cailleen ruadh.

1324.

+)Note. The accidental is supplied from another version of this tune. Ed.

Do Cailín deas ruaḋ.

(County of Donegal.) From Wᵐ. Allingham.

1325.

A Cailín doṅ deas na gcíaċa bána.

or "O pretty brown girl of the white breasts".

From Mac Mahon.

1326.

+)Note. The manuscript has no ♭ in these three places. Ed.

Or The pretty brown girl.

Caílín ʋeaɼ ʋoñ.

A Connaught tune.

?

Caílín ʋeaɼ ʋoñ.

Note. A variant of the preceding. Ed.

Note. The signature should probably be two sharps. Ed.

Oómnall ó ʒɼé.

Dómnall na Spéine.

1331.

Dómnall óg.

Andante.   From Kate Keane, Decr 12th 1854.

1332.

Dómnall óg.

1333.

Cunnla.

1334.

Ta mba ora.

1335.

Leaba clúim 'r córdaíde.

A bed of feathers and ropes. From E. Currey.

1336.

bíveaũ tú fav' a-muiż.

1337.

Cill muire na zcrann.

Allegretto.

1338.

Paddy O'Snap.

1339.

Note. A variant of the preceding. Ed.

336

1340. Nuair a teigimre féin go dtí an t-aonac. Andante.

1341. Nuair a teigim go tig an tabaine.

1342. Ir beag liom a treig.

1343. Sigle a grád. Andante.

+) Note Another version has D♭ in these places. Ed.

1344. Sliab mór.

Slíab mór.

From Coneely.

1345.

Note. A variant of the preceding. Ed.

Is buačaill bó 7 caoraċ.

1346.

Siúbal a ġráo.

From Mrs Harte.

1347.

A ġéġa cumain.

1348.

338

Ḋáıṙe na mḃán-ġlac.

1349.

Note. This tune appears elsewhere, in ⅜ time, one tone lower, and with four flats in the signature. Ed.

Cóta mór rtróċaıġte.

1350.

Ḋoḋa ḃeaṙ níġ Ḋúḃḋa.

1351.

Ḋoḋa ḃeaṙ ní Ḋúḃḋa.

1352.

Oromaṅa na mḃán-ċnoc.

1353.

Máire buitlér.

1354.

Note. Another version (From John Daly's Old MS.) has E♭ throughout. Ed.

Péarla ḋeas an t-sléiḃe.

1355.

Note. See "The roving pedlar" № 360 of which this tune is a variant. Ed.

Pis air an iarta.

1356.

340

Ó Reggi an čúil báin.

1357.

Note. The D and G sharps seem erroneous. Ed.

Cailín beg na luačraó.

1358.

Note. This tune appears again (from Frank Keane) in E♭, but in $\frac{6}{8}$ time. Petrie has pencilled against it "Should be in $\frac{2}{4}$." In this setting the sixth bar appears thus:- Ed.

Cailín ag buaint luačra.

1359.

Áitne bán.

1360. Andante.

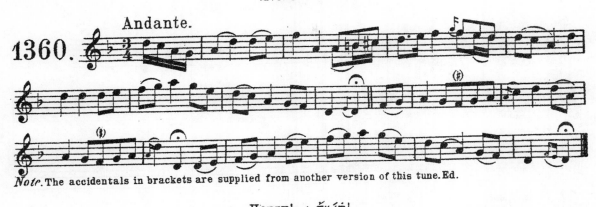

Note. The accidentals in brackets are supplied from another version of this tune. Ed.

Henry! a ġráḋ!

1361. Moderato.

Sléiḃte Féiḋlime.

1362. Andante.   Phelim Mountains. set by Forde from Mr. Pigot's MSS.

Note. The other version of this tune "The Phelim Mountains" has a G♯ throughout. See No. 385. Ed.

Caileaċ an t-súṫa.

1363.

Caitleaċ an t-ṗúṙa.

1364. Lively.

Daḃlaḋ ní Ḋoḃnaláin.

1365.

+)Another version has B♭ in these places. Ed.

bí liom: bí!

1366. Gaily. A Clare spinning tune. From F. Keane.

Ím bím bob-a-ṗú.

1367. Allegro. A Clare spinning tune. From F. Keane.

Ím bím bob-a-ṗú, ṡóṗ' a ṁíle ṡṙáḋ!

1368.

CHORUS.

Ím bím bob-a-pú.

1369.

CHORUS.

[Lacuna.]

CHORUS.

Note. A. variant of the preceding. Ed.

Dúprín óige.

From Miss Ross.

1370.

An veay an buačaill an páiroín.

From Teige Mac Mahon.

1371.

CHORUS.

bárr na craoíbe cúbarta.

From O' Neill's Collection.

1372.

A Ḋáiṛe 'ṛ a ṁúṛnín!

From Father Walsh.

1373.

A Ḋáiṛe! a ṛúin!

as in Mr. Pigott's collection. tune corrected by G. P.

1374.

A Ḋáiṛe! a Rúin!

1375.

Note. A variant of preceding. Ed.

A Ḋáiṛe! a Rúin!

1376.

Note. Another variant of No 1374. Ed.

A Ḋáire! a ṁúin!

1377.

Ġiolla an ḃiaṁoir.

1378.

+) Another version has E♮ here. Ed.

Spailpín! ṁúin!

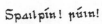

1379.

Note. This tune also occurs with a♯ in the signature. Ed.

Cúṁaḋ Eóġan Rúaiḋ.

1380.

+) Another version has E♮ here. Ed.

bacaċ mire.

1384.

Dómnallín an ċlúmaiġ.

1382.

I otúiṙ an t-ṙaṁṙa.

1383.

An cnoicín ḟṙaoiġ.

1384.

An ᵹaṙḃ-ċnoicín ḟraoiḃ.

Inᵹen Śaḋḃ ó'n mḃáinᵻeċ.

"Ᵹlis'ᵻ ainm.

An ᵹiolla ᵹrúama.

An' ᵹiolla ᵹṗúama.

From the Revd. J. Goodman. 30. Oct. 63.

Andante.

1389.

✣ *Note.* A variant of the preceding. Ed.

An ᵹiolla ᵹṗúama.

1390.

✣ *Note.* Petrie calls this a modern air or Nº 138. Ed.

Ɗála buíꝺe.

1391.

báṛꝺa an ḃṗíṛꝺín leaṫaiṛ.

Gaily.

1392.

Táimṛe tinn.

From O'Neil's collection·

1393.

350

Iṡ cruaġ mar ċonairc mé aen bean a-riaṁ.

1398.

+ *Note.* Petrie says "this seems another setting of the preceding. Ed."

Iṡ buaċaillín beġ óġ mé a ċuġ mór-ġean do Nellí bán.

„I'm a young little boy that has given great love to Nelly ban." **From Margaret Hickey.**

1399.

Níḟi mé air an mbaile ṡeo aċt bliaḋain aġuṡ trí lá.

I am in this town only one year and three days. **From P. Mac Dowell, Esq.**

1400.

+ Another version has this bar thus: Ed.

Péarla an ċúil ċraobaiġ.

From Mr Joyce & Mary Madden.

1401.

This air is also called "Pearla buidhe oir." by Mr Joyce (Petrie's note.)

The Pearl of the yellow road.

Pépla an bótaiṗ buíde.

From Mr Flatley.

1402.

Pépla an ċúil ómṗa.

1403.

An páiṗṗín ḟíoṅ.

As sung in Clare. T. Mac Mahon.

1404.

CHORUS.

(♮)

(♭)

An páiṗṗín ḟíoṅ.

As sung in Kerry. From Father Walsh's MS.

1405.

CHORUS.

(♮)

Tá 'na lá.

From Mr Joyce.

1411.

From a Limerick Woman, in Dublin.

"Tá(1) na lá."

P. Joyce.

Allegretto.

1412.

CHORUS.

Note. To the Nurse tune (No. 1014) Petrie has added a pencil note, "See Ta na la and Mr. Joyce's lullaby." The two lullabys from Mr. Joyce are No. 1008 and 1011 in the present edition. Ed.

Tá 'na lá.

1413.

CHORUS.

Hugh O'Beirne. Different Version.

Eilig geal ciúin.

From Frank Keane.

1414.

Note. Petrie had orginally written bar 3 thus but afterward erased the notes. They should probably be as in the last bar but one. Ed.

354

Tá gleaṅ 4 ḃur ṅḋeaṛ i ṡcṛíc Éiḃiṛ.

From F. Keane.

1415.

Aon 'ṛ ḋo na píobaiṛeáċta.

"The ace and deuce of pipering" – a set dance.

From Mr Joyce.

1416.

Stóiṛín mo ċroíḋe!

1417.

Note. The variants are supplied from another version of this tune. Ed.

Ní 'ṛ ġaḃ ṛé ḋ'Éóċaill.

From O'Neill's collection.

1418.

Uilliam mac "Peter".

From O' Neill's collection.

1419.

Níl agam 'r an raoġal.

From O' Neill's collection.

1420.

Cnoc ġréine.

From O' Neill's collection.

1421.

Jack an cuí, leat?

From O' Neill's collection.

1422

+)*Note.* The sharp is supplied from a second version of this tune. Ed.

Ná ṫṙóiċ mo léine.

1423.

A clan march.

Feaḋaoil an fiolair.

With spirit.

1424.

Note. This is a version of "The Eagle's Whistle." See No. 305 and 306. Ed.

Ancient clan march.

Ó ṙo! 'ré ṫo ḃeaṫa a ḃaile.

March time.

1425.

Note. Compare this with No. 983. Ed.

beir leat mé.

Affettuoso.

1426.

2 cailín vear óig an ṫúinín uaiṫne!

From John O'Daly's Kilrush MS.

1427.

Sláinte Ríóg Philip.

1428.

A Ḋáire! is deas do ġáire; nó
Caitilín na Rodaire, plúr na mban.

From Frank Keane.

Called also "Kathleen na Rudderigh, the flower of women," see setting by Mr. Mc. Dowell.

Andante.

1429.

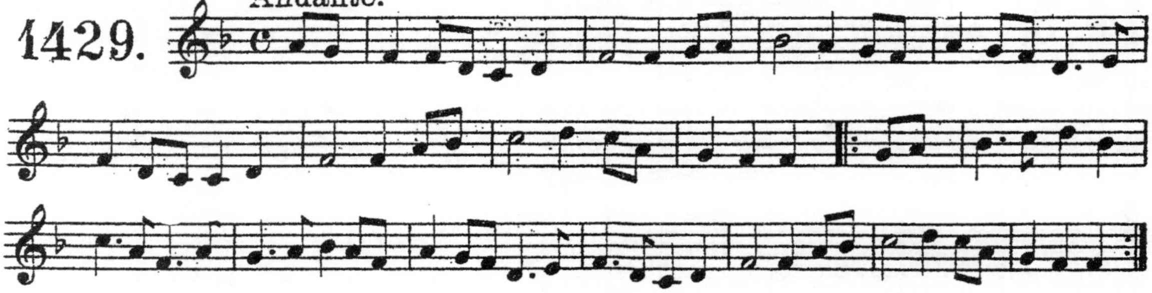

A Ḋáire! is deas do ġáire.

Andante.

From Frank Keane.

1430.

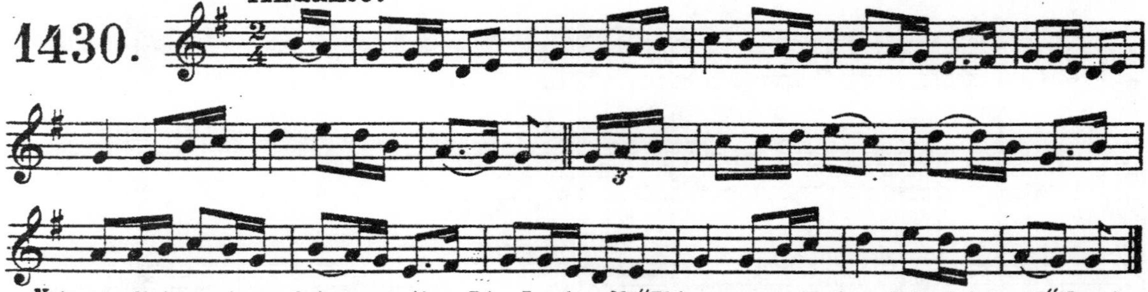

Note. A slight variant of the preceding. Ed. Petrie adds "This seems to be the original form of "My ain kind dearie." See No. 640. Ed.

Baile Ḃeaċáin.

1431.

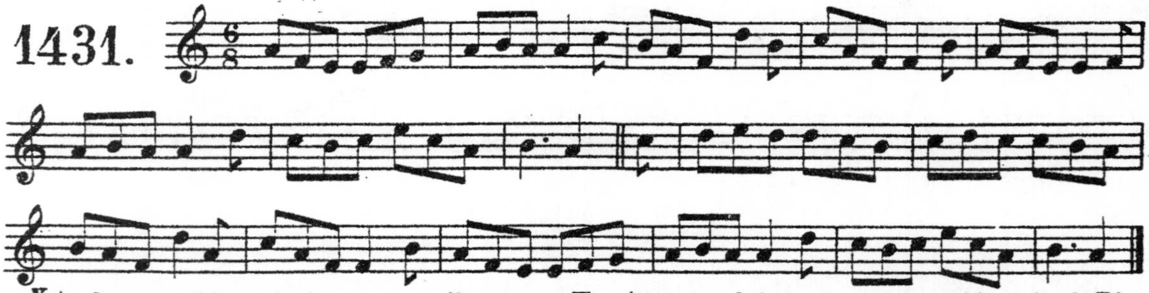

Note. Compare this with the two preceding tunes. The signature of three sharps is probably omitted. Ed.

Nuair a d'eirig an ċaile air maidin.

From Frank Keane.

1432.

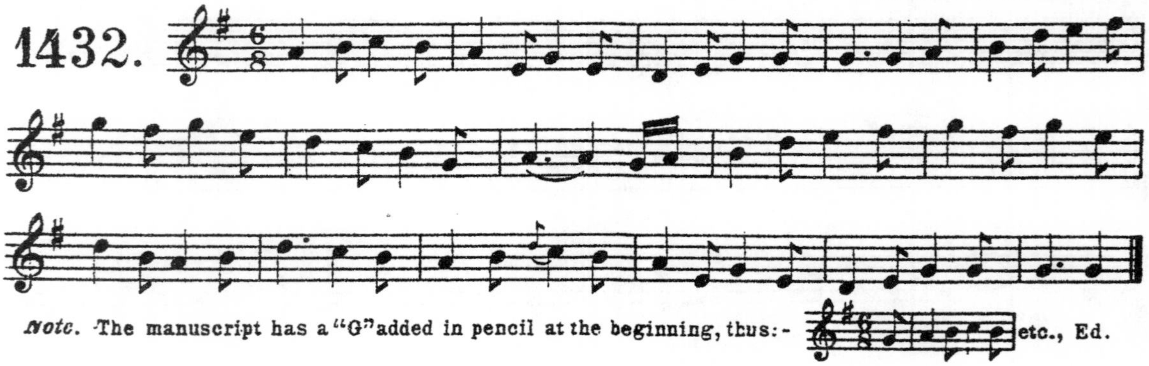

Note. The manuscript has a "G" added in pencil at the beginning, thus:- etc., Ed.

Opomanaó na manla, nó Dolly bpeáğ Wúğent.

From Frank Keane.

1433.

+)Another version has a ♭ in these places. Ed.

Dolly bpeáğ Wúğent.

From Frank Keane.

Andante.

1434.

Note. A variant of the preceding. Ed.

Dáipe an bapbpéa.

From Frank Keane.

Allegretto.

1435.

CHORUS.

Tamall oá pabap-pa.

Andante.

1436.

Advice to a young man in choosing a wife. From Galway. P. Mac D.

Andante.

1437.

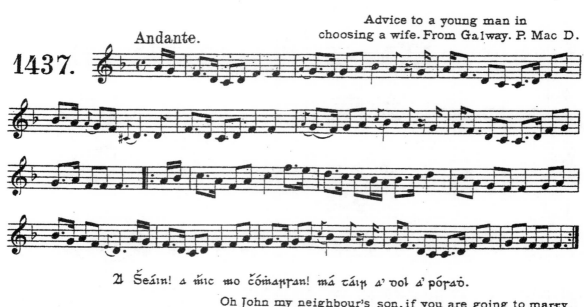

2l Šeáin! a ṁic mo cóṁarṙan! má táir a' ḋol a' póraḋ.

Oh John my neighbour's son, if you are going to marry.

1438.

Note. A variant of the preceding. Ed.

Do caṫúġaḋ 7 huṗluṙ do ċonnac mé.

Co. Limerick. From P. Mac Dowell.

1439.

Éiriġ rí a-ḃaile, 7 aḃair naċ raċaiṁ-ṡe léi.

From P. MacDowell Esq.

1440.

✣ *Note.* See No. 594. Ed.

Capa ḃániġ.

Set from L. O'Brien by Mr Joyce
August 1854.

1441.

✤ *Note.* See No. 368. Ed.

Do Ġráḋ! naċ feárr(a) ḋúiṅ fuireċtaiṅ.

Had not we better wait, my dear.

1442.

Raḋaire iṅ ḃaiġniṡ.

From „A collection of the most celebrated Irish tunes."
Printed and sold by John and Wᵐ Neal. Christ church yard.

1443.

✤ *Note.* Petrie indicates the same source for his copy of "Patrick Sarsfield." No. 311. Ed.

Aꞃ mo "Ramble" ꝺam, ꞇꞃáꞇ nóna.

1444.

+ *Note.* Petrie has probably omitted two flats in the signature.　See, "Rise up young William Reilly" No. 510. Ed.

Ó'Ðıa ꞃú, a Ṡeáṁaın!

O God John. See the Gaelic air "oran an avig" & Bunting's "A chieftain" &c

From Frank Keane & Kate Keane.

1445.

Ꞡꞃáꞇ ı ꞃan ól.

1446.

huꞃꞃa ꝺan Ðáıṁın.

1447.

Ḋaroin ⱥíḃin coir raíḃ an ġleaña.

Slow.

1448.

Ḋaroin áíḃiñ coir raíḃ an ġleaña.

From Mary Madden.'54.

1449.

✛ *Note.* A variant of the preceding. Ed.

ḃáṗṗ an rṙléiḃ.

or. 'The top of the mountain, an ancient dance tune.

1450.

✛ *Note.* This tune also occurs with no ♯ in the signature. Ed.

Is áíḃiñ ro(ṡ) na héiñiṁ.

Andante.

1451.

Cill Caiṛ; no ban-ṫiġeṛna íḃeaċ.

1452.

Spíanán ban Éiṛeḃ.

1453.

÷ Another version gives C♯ and D♯ here. Ed.

baile Ṗáṗaic.

1454. Andante con spirito.

Spáiṅe Ḋaél.

1455.

Chorus.

÷ *Note.* See "Poor old Granua Weal" No. 790. Ed.

Ʒeaрán buíƌe.

From Miss Ross.

1456.

An Ʒeaрán buíƌe.

1457.

An Ʒeaрán buíƌe.

As in a MS. of 1780.

1458.

✝ *Note.* See. "The yellow Horse" No. 577 of which this is a slight variant. Ed.

Tá mé caillte.

1459.

✠ *Note.* The other version of this tune, "I'm lost without her," has no sharp in the signature, but the notes marked + are sharpened. Ed.

Siúd ort, a máṫair mo ċéile!

"Here's a health to the mother-in-law."

Father Walsh's M.S.

1460.

Slán 7 beṅaċt lé buaḋarṫaiḃ an t-saoġail.

1461.

+*Note.* Another version has no ♮ in these places.

Slán 7 beaṅaċt lé búaipeaṁ an t-saoiġil.

"Goodbye, and my blessing to the troubles of the world." From Father Walsh.

1462.

✠ *Note.* Petrie adds a pencil note "I have another set of this in some book."

Slán agar beannact lé búaineam an traigil.

Allegretto.

Set from Joseph Martin, by W. Joyce.

1463.

✛ *Note.* The Flats are supplied from another version of this tune. Ed.

huir-eó! mo leanb.

Andante.

1464.

✛ *Note.* This is a second setting of No. 1016. Ed.

huir-eó! mo leanb.

Allegro.

1465.

✛ *Note.* This is a third (March) setting of No. 1016. Ed.

366

Note. For other Hymn tunes & caoines see Nos 1018–1050. Ed.

luġen Ṡaïöḃ ó'n ṁḃeanreaċ.

1471.

A ḋoċtúir ḋílir!

1472.

Note. See "O Johnny, dearest Johnny" etc. Nº 693. Ed.

Ḋúna ḃána. ḃorċa. ḃoṅ.

A mock scolding spinning tune. T. Mac Mahon.

Allegretto.

1473.

Lúpa, lúpa. nó ḃá lúpa.

A mock scolding spinning song. From Mac Mahon & Curry.

1474.

Ḋail leó léṗó.

A spinning tune.

Allegretto.

1475.

Aṅ maiḋiṅ ḋia luain iṣeaḋ ḋ'ḟáġaṁ aṅ cluain.

1476.

Aṅ ćeaṅtaṛ Cluaiṅ-na-Ḋeala, 7 Caṛṛaiġ-na-Riṁṛe.

1477.

Note. A variant of the preceding Ed.

Sláṅ 7 beaṅaċt lé búaḋṛaiḃ aṅ t-ṣaoġail.

1478.

Note. See N⁰ 1463. Ed.

Ḋéṅṗaiḋ mé "cuilt" ḋo'm ḟeaṅ "bṛiste".

1479.

Note. Petrie adds, "The same as 'The Tanner's wife etc.' and "This time twelve-month I married." Ed.

Oá ʒcappaide bean canapaide liompa.

"If I should meet a Tanner's wife."

1480.

Note. A variant of the preceding. Ed.

Suid aũ po, a ṁúippín! láiṁ liom.

Set her near me, my Murneen.

1481.

Suid aũ po, a ṁúippín! láiṁ liom.

"Sit here, O Murneen, near me."

1482.

Note. The signature should obviously be 3 flats. The first 6 notes of the tune have a pencil alteration in the M S. lowering each one a tone. Compare the preceding tune. Ed.

Ʒpáð mo ċpoide-pe.

Andante.

1483.

Iɼ caiłín beaʒ óʒ mé.

1484.

372

"Humours of Kilkenny." Your bag is handsome my boy.   From MS. book of 1770.

1485.

+ Petrie adds in a note the following three bars as an alternative
                            or correction here:-

"Here's a health to the mother in law."   Father Walsh's MS.

1486.

or, Will you come home with me.   From Paddy Conneely, & other Pipers.

1487.

"O little Mary, what has happened thee."   From T. Mac Mahon.

1488.

373

At the yellow Boreen lives the secret of my heart.

1489.

From T. Mac Mahon.

Note. Compare this tune with the preceding. Ed.

1490.

From T. Mac Mahon.

1491.

From T. Mac Mahon.

CHORUS.

Oh Mary if my advice you take.

1492.

From T. Mac Mahon.

374

bí mire lá a oul go luimneác.

I was one day going to Limerick.

1493.

CHORUS.

Cia ciofeao riú Oaipéo ní h-áille 4 maioin oia Oáipt go moc.

Lawsy Dulh.

From Mac Mahon.

1494.

Note. The M S. has a pencil note, "There's not in the wide world a valley so sweet."Ed.

Plúipín na mban oon óg.

The little flow'r of brown-haired girls.

From Mac Mahon.

1495.

2l buacaillíoe óga! an baile reo.

1496.

Lá lé Páopac biora.

"On Patrick's day I was in my element!"

From Mac Mahon.

1497.

Do ċeaṁaiġ an Róirteaċ bó ar an aonaċ.

From Mac Mahon.

1498.

Ḋá ir maiṫ leat.

1499.

Ġráḋ mo ċroíḋe.

From Teig Mac Mahon.

1500.

CHORUS.

Ar truaġ ġan mac an ṁaoir aġam.

From Mac Mahon.

1501.

376

Tá caiłín aṗ an ḃṗiaḋ.

From Mac Mahon.

1502.

Ꝺo ḃ. ʈuiᵹeann Murphy.

From P. J. O' Reilly Esq.

1503.

Óċ! a ḃean a' ʈiᵹe!

"O woman of the house is not that pleasant?" A white-boy march.

From T. Mc M. & E. Curry.

1504.

Note. A variant of Nº 994. Ed.

Tá boʈáinín aᵹam-ṡa.

"I have a cottage on the verge of the mountain."

T. Mc Mahon.

1505.

Do čuaðar-ra a n-iar-čar &c.

"I went to the west to look for a wife."

1506.

Ir búačaillín og &c.

From T. Mac Mahon.

1507.

Cearc agar coileač a ð'imčiġ lé čéile.

From T. Mac Mahon.

1508.

Cearc agar coileač a ð'imčiġ lé čéile.

Gaily.

1509.

béḟḟaiṁ ḋuiṫ iaṙċaṙ aᵹ iaṙṙaiḋ.

"I would advise you to pass over the boundary."

From T. Mac Mahon.

1510.

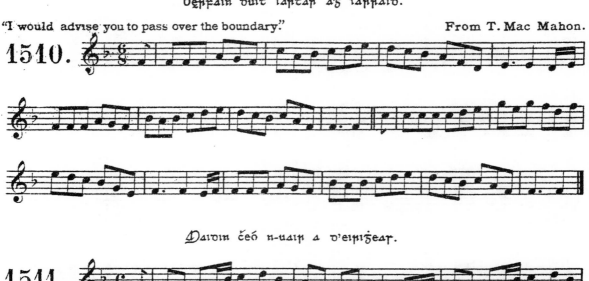

Ɗaiṁiṅ ċeó n-uaiṙ a ḃ'eiṙiᵹeaṫ.

1511.

Note. Petrie adds "See Hardiman's & Joyce's sets of this." See "The Morning Star" Nᵒ 895. Ed.

Ɗaiṁiṅ ċeó n-uaiṙ a ḃ'eiṙiᵹeaṫ.

1512.

Note. A variant of the preceding. Ed.

Ɗaɩoɩɲ ċeóòaċ ɲuaɩɲ ɒ'éɩɲɩẑeaɲ.

Andante.   From Mr. Hardiman.

1513.

2l ccuɩṁɩɲ leaⱃ?

                                            From Mary Madden.

1514.

Note. Petrie adds the following in pencil:— "Remember thee, yes while there's life in this heart." Ed.

2l ⱃá ɲṁóɩlíɲ ɩ ẑcɩúṁaɩɲ &c.

1515.

beaɲ a ɓaɩɲ ɒɩlleaɲc.

1516.

2l ċaɩlɩuɲíɲ ɩⱃ maẑaɩö &c.

1517.

380

Uċ! óċ on! aṛṛ an ꞇannaiṛe buíḋe.

Och och one, said the yellow tanner.

1518.

Iṛ iomaḃa yeóman malluiġċe ꝺo ċill a ḃóġaḃ.

From Mary Madden.

1519.

An ṗélꞇan leanḃaċ.

The childlike star.

1520.

CHORUS.

Note. This and the preceding tune are variants of "John Doe" Nº 738. They are given by Petrie as "second setting" and "third setting" respectively of that tune, which occurs several times in his manuscript. Ed.

Tá an teine gan coigilt.

1521.

Dá bfágfaiñ-re Sióbán 'r a cófra.

Form T. MacMahon.

1522.

Dá mbeaó lán páirce &c.

1523.

Tá gleañ beg vraíóeáča.

There is a little enchanted glen that I know.

1524.

382

383

A lorg mo ṫamain.

"To look for my calves I sent my child."
Andante.

1529.

From M. Madden. 1854.

Ar ċuairiṫe na ngamna &c.

From T. Mac Mahon.

1530.

(b)

Note. A variant of the preceding. Ed.

Dómnall ua Dilleáin.

1531.

384

An bean úc ríop y buaé an c-rrucáin, reó cú beó.

1532.

CHORUS.

Héipíñ.

1533.

An ṁráṁ naé mbíṁean i láṁaip.

or, Out of sight, out out of mind.

1534.

Ceaṅ ouḃ óiliṛ.

The new mountain road.

A Connaught Jigg.

1535.

Ouaḷín ouḃaċ.

Allegretto.

1536.

'S a ṁúṛṅín óiliṛ! Iṛ tú mo leaṅḃ.

1537.

'S a ṁúṛṅín óiliṛ!

Allegretto.

1538.

Luimneać. (Limerick)

(Ossian's Poems.)

1539.

Cronánać.

Andante.

(Ossian's Poems.)

1540.

Eóġan cóir.

1541.

Dáire níġ hEiḋin.

1542.

Ingean Séain uí Catarain.

1543.

Luaċ mo léṫpíne.

1544.

Cuippim-re ċuġuṫ-ra an rcapbán reóil.

A weaving tune of the Cº of Clare.

1545.

Note. Petrie adds "See F. Keane's Set." Ed.

Ⱃic ó! mo ġráṫ.

1546.

Síżlè níż żamna.

1547.

Síżlè níż żaròpe.

Set in the C? of Londonderry.

1548.

bacač na cleaċa.

A Connemara tune.

1549.

Note: + Another version has 𝄢 in these two places. Ed.

390

Súigte buíóe.

Mr. Joyce. From L. O' Brien.

1554.

bɼaé! ná póg.

From P. Coneely.

1555.

2l čailín bíg úaɼail na gɼúaige bɼeág buíóe.

Andante.

From F. Keane.

1556.

Ⅎ čɑilín bíᵹ uɑꞃɑil nɑ ᵹꞃúɑiᵹe bꞃeɑ́ᵹ buíɗe.

From Frank Keane. 10. Sep. 54.

1557.

Note. A variant of the preceding. Ed.

Slán iomlán ꝺo'n áit ɑ ꞃɑbɑꞃ.

From F. Keane.

1558.

(+ Another version has E♮ here. Ed.

Ⅎiꞃ mo ᵹɑbáil tꞃé bleáᴛ Ⅽliaᴛ ꝺɑm.

From L O' Brien, by Mr. Joyce.

1559.

Ƶeɑᴛín aiꞃ cꞃúꝺ.

From P. Carew's MS.

1560.

392

Ⴆeⴆⲅⲓⲛ ⲁⲓⲣ ⲥⲣⲩⲃ.

From P. Carew's MSS.

1561.

Note. A variant of the preceding. Ed.

Ⲇⲟⲣ ⲥⲗⲩⲁⲛⲁ. Set by Mr. Joyce from Lewis O'Brien, Coolfree, C.° of Limerick. Aug. 1854.

1562.

Note. The two variants in this tune are supplied from a second version. Ed.

Ⴆⲁⲣⲣ ⲛⲁ ⲥⲣⲁⲟⲓⳝe ⲥⴋⲙⲣⲁ.

1563.

Ⴎⲛ ⲣⲉⲁⲛⲃⲩⲓⲛⲉ ⲥⲣⲟⴋ.

Allegretto.   Mr. Joyce from J. Martin.

1564.

Iṡ inġean eiġpe mé ġan ʼooḃc

Andante.

From Frank Keane.

1565.

bean ouḃ óʼn ṙliaḃ.

The black-haired woman from the mountain.

Set from J. Martin, by Mr Joyce.

Andante.

1566.

bean ouḃ óʼn ṙliaḃ.

Andante.

1567.

Note. A slight variant of the preceding. Ed.

394

bean oub ó'n ṛliaḃ.

The dark-haired woman from the mountain.

A Mayo Air.
From P. Joyce. March 1864.

Andante.

1568.

A "Landlady" na páiṛṫe!
Ταḃαiṛ cáṛt eile oo'n ṁiġ ṛeo a-ṛteaċ.

From Mr Hickey.

1569.

Siḃéil ni Ḃṛiain.

Andante.

1570.

A Ógánaiġ ṛo ḃṛeáġ! cáṛ' ċoᴅail ᴅú a-ṛéiṛ?
nó, A ḃuaċaill an ċúil ᴅualaiġ

Allegretto.

From M. Madden.

1571.

Ógánaiġ an ċúil ᴅualaiġ!

1572.

Do ċṛeaċ 'ṛ mo ḃiċ,'ṛ aṛ cloiġᴅe an ᴣalaṛ an ᴣṛáᴅ.

Allegretto.

From Frank Keane.

1573.

Do ċṛeaċ iṛ mo lᴇn ᴣan kitty aᴣuṛ mé.

From T. MacMahon.

1574.

Do ċreaċ a'ṛ mo ḃíaċaiṛ.

Andante.

Mr. Joyce From Jo. Martin.

1575.

✠ *Note.* Another version has E♮ in these places. Ed.

Do ċreaċ 'ṛ mo ḃíaċaiṛ.

Andante.

1576.

✠ *Note.* Another version has no♯ in these places. Ed.

boġaṛíḋ ḟuṛta.

1577.

Ṡreaḋaḋ aiṛ an nṡṛáḋ ṛo aṛ maiṛṡ aiṛ mbionn.

A scorching to this (love), woe be him who it is upon.

From Mary Madden.

1578.

A County of Louth air. From J. Tighe.

1579.

† *Note.* The Phonetic English title to this air is written thus: "Un Killau creggam." Ed.

Péapla an bpollaig báin.

1580.

O r céaomíle ríán oón áir ap ċooail mé péir,   Sín - re zo

ráin   láṁ le   bṗuinzeall mo cléib Do   ċuip mé mo láṁ i láp a

bṗollaiz r a   ceib, S oo puz ri - re zṗáò beaz lao zan cuiṗṗe oom féin.

Nuaip a o'eipiz an caile aip maioin.

1581.

An ṗmaċoín cṗón.

"The brown little Mallet."

1582.

Note. A pencil note to this title says "or Roll of Tobacco." Ed.

Dover Opera, Choral and Lieder Scores

Mozart, Wolfgang Amadeus, DON GIOVANNI: COMPLETE ORCHESTRAL SCORE. Full score that contains everything from the original version, along with later arias, recitatives, and duets added to original score for Vienna performance. Peters edition. Study score. 468pp. 9⅜ x 12¼. (Available in U.S. only) 23026-0

Mozart, Wolfgang Amadeus, THE MAGIC FLUTE (DIE ZAUBERFLÖTE) IN FULL SCORE. Authoritative C. F. Peters edition of Mozart's brilliant last opera still widely popular. Includes all the spoken dialogue. 226pp. 9 x 12. 24783-X

Mozart, Wolfgang Amadeus, THE MARRIAGE OF FIGARO: COMPLETE SCORE. Finest comic opera ever written. Full score, beautifully engraved, includes passages often cut in other editions. Peters edition. Study score. 448pp. 9⅜ x 12¼. (Available in U.S. only) 23751-6

Mozart, Wolfgang Amadeus, REQUIEM IN FULL SCORE. Masterpiece of vocal composition, among the most recorded and performed works in the repertoire. Authoritative edition published by Breitkopf & Härtel, Wiesbaden. 203pp. 8⅜ x 11¼. 25311-2

Offenbach, Jacques, OFFENBACH'S SONGS FROM THE GREAT OPERETTAS. Piano, vocal (French text) for 38 most popular songs: *Orphée, Belle Hélène, Vie Parisienne, Duchesse de Gérolstein*, others. 21 illustrations. 195pp. 9 x 12. 23341-3

Puccini, Giacomo, LA BOHÈME IN FULL SCORE. Authoritative Italian edition of one of the world's most beloved operas. English translations of list of characters and instruments. 416pp. 8⅜ x 11¼. (Not available in United Kingdom, France, Germany or Italy) 25477-1

Rossini, Gioacchino, THE BARBER OF SEVILLE IN FULL SCORE. One of the greatest comic operas ever written, reproduced here directly from the authoritative score published by Ricordi. 464pp. 8⅜ x 11¼. 26019-4

Schubert, Franz, COMPLETE SONG CYCLES. Complete piano, vocal music of *Die Schöne Müllerin, Die Winterreise, Schwanengesang*. Also Drinker English singing translations. Breitkopf & Härtel edition. 217pp. 9⅜ x 12¼. 22649-2

Schubert, Franz, SCHUBERT'S SONGS TO TEXTS BY GOETHE. Only one-volume edition of Schubert's Goethe songs from authoritative Breitkopf & Härtel edition, plus all revised versions. New prose translation of poems. 84 songs. 256pp. 9⅜ x 12¼. 23752-4

Schubert, Franz, 59 FAVORITE SONGS. "Der Wanderer," "Ave Maria," "Hark, Hark, the Lark," and 56 other masterpieces of lieder reproduced from the Breitkopf & Härtel edition. 256pp. 9⅜ x 12¼. 24849-6

Schumann, Robert, SELECTED SONGS FOR SOLO VOICE AND PIANO. Over 100 of Schumann's greatest lieder, set to poems by Heine, Goethe, Byron, others. Breitkopf & Härtel edition. 248pp. 9⅜ x 12¼. 24202-1

Strauss, Richard, DER ROSENKAVALIER IN FULL SCORE. First inexpensive edition of great operatic masterpiece, reprinted complete and unabridged from rare, limited Fürstner edition (1910) approved by Strauss. 528pp. 9⅜ x 12¼. (Available in U.S. only) 25498-4

Strauss, Richard, DER ROSENKAVALIER: VOCAL SCORE. Inexpensive edition reprinted directly from original Fürstner (1911) edition of vocal score. Verbal text, vocal line and piano "reduction." 448pp. 8⅜ x 11¼. (Not available in Europe or the United Kingdom) 25501-8

Strauss, Richard, SALOME IN FULL SCORE. Atmospheric color predominates in composer's first great operatic success. Definitive Fürstner score, now extremely rare. 352pp. 9⅜ x 12¼. (Available in U.S. only) 24208-0

Verdi, Giuseppe, AÏDA IN FULL SCORE. Verdi's glorious, most popular opera, reprinted from an authoritative edition published by G. Ricordi, Milan. 448pp. 9 x 12. 26172-7

Verdi, Giuseppe, FALSTAFF. Verdi's last great work, his first and only comedy. Complete unabridged score from original Ricordi edition. 480pp. 8⅜ x 11¼. 24017-7

Verdi, Giuseppe, OTELLO IN FULL SCORE. The penultimate Verdi opera, his tragic masterpiece. Complete unabridged score from authoritative Ricordi edition, with Front Matter translated. 576pp. 8¼ x 11. 25040-7

Verdi, Giuseppe, REQUIEM IN FULL SCORE. Immensely popular with choral groups and music lovers. Republication of edition published by C. F. Peters, Leipzig. Study score. 204pp. 9⅜ x 12¼. (Available in U.S. only) 23682-X

Wagner, Richard, DAS RHEINGOLD IN FULL SCORE. Complete score, clearly reproduced from B. Schott's authoritative edition. New translation of German Front Matter. 328pp. 9 x 12. 24925-5

Wagner, Richard, DIE MEISTERSINGER VON NÜRNBERG. Landmark in history of opera, in complete vocal and orchestral score of one of the greatest comic operas. C. F. Peters edition, Leipzig. Study score. 823pp. 8⅛ x 11. 23276-X

Wagner, Richard, DIE WALKÜRE. Complete orchestral score of the most popular of the operas in the Ring Cycle. Reprint of the edition published in Leipzig by C. F. Peters, ca. 1910. Study score. 710pp. 8⅜ x 11¼. 23566-1

Wagner, Richard, THE FLYING DUTCHMAN IN FULL SCORE. Great early masterpiece reproduced directly from limited Weingartner edition (1896), incorporating Wagner's revisions. Text, stage directions in English, German, Italian. 432pp. 9⅜ x 12¼. 25629-4

Wagner, Richard, GÖTTERDÄMMERUNG. Full operatic score, first time available in U.S. Reprinted directly from rare 1877 first edition. 615pp. 9⅜ x 12¼. 24250-1

Wagner, Richard, LOHENGRIN IN FULL SCORE. Wagner's most accessible opera. Reproduced from first engraved edition (Breitkopf & Härtel, 1887). 295pp. 9⅜ x 12¼. 24335-4

Wagner, Richard, PARSIFAL IN FULL SCORE. Composer's deeply personal treatment of the legend of the Holy Grail, renowned for splendid music, glowing orchestration. C. F. Peters edition. 592pp. 8⅛ x 11. 25175-6

Wagner, Richard, SIEGFRIED IN FULL SCORE. *Siegfried*, third opera of Wagner's famous Ring Cycle, is reproduced from first edition (1876). 439pp. 9⅜ x 12¼. 24456-3

Wagner, Richard, TANNHAUSER IN FULL SCORE. Reproduces the original 1845 full orchestral and vocal score as slightly amended in 1847. Included is the ballet music for Act I written for the 1861 Paris production. 576pp. 8⅜ x 11¼. 24649-3

Wagner, Richard, TRISTAN UND ISOLDE. Full orchestral score with complete instrumentation. Study score. 655pp. 8⅛ x 11. 22915-7

von Weber, Carl Maria, DER FREISCHÜTZ. Full orchestral score to first Romantic opera, forerunner to Wagner and later developments. Still very popular. Study score, including full spoken text. 203pp. 9 x 12. 23449-5

Wolf, Hugo, THE COMPLETE MÖRIKE SONGS. Splendid settings to music of 53 German poems by Eduard Mörike, including "Der Tambour," "Elfenlied," and "Verborganheit." New prose translations. 208pp. 9⅜ x 12¼. 24380-X

Wolf, Hugo, SPANISH AND ITALIAN SONGBOOKS. Total of 90 songs by great 19th-century master of the genre. Reprint of authoritative C. F. Peters edition. New Translations of German texts. 256pp. 9⅜ x 12¼. 26156-5

Available from your music dealer or write for free Music Catalog to
Dover Publications, Inc., Dept. MUBI, 31 East 2nd Street, Mineola, NY 11501
Visit us online at www.doverpublications.com

Dover Opera, Choral and Lieder Scores

Bach, Johann Sebastian, ELEVEN GREAT CANTATAS. Full vocal-instrumental score from Bach-Gesellschaft edition. *Christ lag in Tödesbanden, Ich hatte viel Bekümmerniss, Jauchhzet Gott in allen Landen,* eight others. Study score. 350pp. 9 χ 12. 23268-9

Bach, Johann Sebastian, MASS IN B MINOR IN FULL SCORE. The crowning glory of Bach's lifework in the field of sacred music and a universal statement of Christian faith, reprinted from the authoritative Bach-Gesellschaft edition. Translation of texts. 320pp. 9 x 12. 25992-7

Bach, Johann Sebastian, SEVEN GREAT SACRED CANTATAS IN FULL SCORE. Seven favorite sacred cantatas. Printed from a clear, modern engraving and sturdily bound; new literal line-for-line translations. Reliable Bach-Gesellschaft edition. Complete German texts. 256pp. 9 x 12. 24950-6

Bach, Johann Sebastian, SIX GREAT SECULAR CANTATAS IN FULL SCORE. Bach's nearest approach to comic opera. *Hunting Cantata, Wedding Cantata, Aeolus Appeased, Phoebus and Pan, Coffee Cantata,* and *Peasant Cantata.* 286pp. 9 x 12. 23934-9

Beethoven, Ludwig van, FIDELIO IN FULL SCORE. Beethoven's only opera, complete in one affordable volume, including all spoken German dialogue. Republication of C. F. Peters, Leipzig edition. 272pp. 9 x 12. 24740-6

Beethoven, Ludwig van, SONGS FOR SOLO VOICE AND PIANO. 71 lieder, including "Adelaide," "Wonne der Wehmuth," "Die ehre Gottes aus der Natur," and famous cycle *An die ferne Geliebta.* Breitkopf & Härtel edition. 192pp. 9 x 12. 25125-X

Bizet, Georges, CARMEN IN FULL SCORE. Complete, authoritative score of perhaps the world's most popular opera, in the version most commonly performed today, with recitatives by Ernest Guiraud. 574pp. 9 x 12. 25820-3

Brahms, Johannes, COMPLETE SONGS FOR SOLO VOICE AND PIANO (two volumes). A total of 113 songs in complete score by greatest lieder writer since Schubert. Series I contains 15-song cycle *Die Schone Magelone;* Series II includes famous "Lullaby." Total of 448pp. 9⅜ x 12¼.
Series I: 23820-2
Series II: 23821-0

Brahms, Johannes, COMPLETE SONGS FOR SOLO VOICE AND PIANO: Series III. 64 songs, published from 1877 to 1886, include such favorites as "Geheimnis," "Alte Liebe," and "Vergebliches Standchen." 224pp. 9 x 12. 23822-9

Brahms, Johannes, COMPLETE SONGS FOR SOLO VOICE AND PIANO: Series IV. 120 songs that complete the Brahms song oeuvre, with sensitive arrangements of 91 folk and traditional songs. 240pp. 9 x 12. 23823-7

Brahms, Johannes, GERMAN REQUIEM IN FULL SCORE. Definitive Breitkopf & Härtel edition of Brahms's greatest vocal work, fully scored for solo voices, mixed chorus and orchestra. 208pp. 9⅜ x 12¼. 25486-0

Debussy, Claude, PELLÉAS ET MÉLISANDE IN FULL SCORE. Reprinted from the E. Fromont (1904) edition, this volume faithfully reproduces the full orchestral-vocal score of Debussy's sole and enduring opera masterpiece. 416pp. 9 x 12. (Available in U.S. only) 24825-9

Debussy, Claude, SONGS, 1880–1904. Rich selection of 36 songs set to texts by Verlaine, Baudelaire, Pierre Louÿs, Charles d'Orleans, others. 175pp. 9 x 12. 24131-9

Fauré, Gabriel, SIXTY SONGS. "Clair de lune," "Apres un reve," "Chanson du pecheur," "Automne," and other great songs set for medium voice. Reprinted from French editions. 288pp. 8⅜ x 11. (Not available in France or Germany) 26534-X

Gilbert, W. S. and Sullivan, Sir Arthur, THE AUTHENTIC GILBERT & SULLIVAN SONGBOOK, 92 songs, uncut, original keys, in piano renderings approved by Sullivan. 399pp. 9 x 12. 23482-7

Gilbert, W. S. and Sullivan, Sir Arthur, HMS PINAFORE IN FULL SCORE. New edition by Carl Simpson and Ephraim Hammett Jones. Some of Gilbert's most clever flashes of wit and a number of Sullivan's most charming melodies in a handsome, authoritative new edition based on original manuscripts and early sources. 256pp. 9 x 12. 42201-1

Gilbert, W. S. and Sullivan, Sir Arthur (Carl Simpson and Ephraim Hammett Jones, eds.), THE PIRATES OF PENZANCE IN FULL SCORE. New performing edition corrects numerous errors, offers performers the choice of two versions of the Act II finale, and gives the first accurate full score of the "Climbing over Rocky Mountain" section. 288pp. 9 x 12. 41891-X

Hale, Philip (ed.), FRENCH ART SONGS OF THE NINETEENTH CENTURY: 39 Works from Berlioz to Debussy. 39 songs from romantic period by 18 composers: Berlioz, Chausson, Debussy (six songs), Gounod, Massenet, Thomas, etc. French text, English singing translation for high voice. 182pp. 9 x 12. (Not available in France or Germany) 23680-3

Handel, George Frideric, GIULIO CESARE IN FULL SCORE. Great Baroque masterpiece reproduced directly from authoritative Deutsche Handelgesellschaft edition. Gorgeous melodies, inspired orchestration. Complete and unabridged. 160pp. 9⅜ x 12¼. 25056-3

Handel, George Frideric, MESSIAH IN FULL SCORE. An authoritative full-score edition of the oratorio that is the best-known, most-beloved, most-performed large-scale musical work in the English-speaking world. 240pp. 9 x 12. 26067-4

Lehar, Franz, THE MERRY WIDOW: Complete Score for Piano and Voice in English. Complete score for piano and voice, reprinted directly from the first English translation (1907) published by Chappell & Co., London. 224pp. 8⅜ x 11¼. (Available in U.S. only) 24514-4

Liszt, Franz, THIRTY SONGS. Selection of extremely worthwhile though not widely-known songs. Texts in French, German, and Italian, all with English translations. Piano, high voice. 144pp. 9 x 12. 23197-6

Monteverdi, Claudio, MADRIGALS: BOOK IV & V. 39 finest madrigals with new line-for-line literal English translations of the poems facing the Italian text. 256pp. 8⅛ x 11. (Available in U.S. only) 25102-0

Moussorgsky, Modest Petrovich, BORIS GODUNOV IN FULL SCORE (Rimsky-Korsakov Version). Russian operatic masterwork in most-recorded, most-performed version. Authoritative Moscow edition. 784pp. 8⅜ x 11¼. 25321-X

Mozart, Wolfgang Amadeus, THE ABDUCTION FROM THE SERAGLIO IN FULL SCORE. Mozart's early comic masterpiece, exactingly reproduced from the authoritative Breitkopf & Härtel edition. 320pp. 9 x 12. 26004-6

Mozart, Wolfgang Amadeus, COSI FAN TUTTE IN FULL SCORE. Scholarly edition of one of Mozart's greatest operas. Da Ponte libretto. Commentary. Preface. Translated Front Matter. 448pp. 9⅜ x 12¼. (Available in U.S. only) 24528-4

Dover Orchestral Scores

Bach, Johann Sebastian, COMPLETE CONCERTI FOR SOLO KEYBOARD AND ORCHESTRA IN FULL SCORE. Bach's seven complete concerti for solo keyboard and orchestra in full score from the authoritative Bach-Gesellschaft edition. 206pp. 9 x 12. 24929-8

Bach, Johann Sebastian, THE SIX BRANDENBURG CONCERTOS AND THE FOUR ORCHESTRAL SUITES IN FULL SCORE. Complete standard Bach-Gesellschaft editions in large, clear format. Study score. 273pp. 9 x 12. 23376-6

Bach, Johann Sebastian, THE THREE VIOLIN CONCERTI IN FULL SCORE. Concerto in A Minor, BWV 1041; Concerto in E Major, BWV 1042; and Concerto for Two Violins in D Minor, BWV 1043. Bach-Gesellschaft editions. 64pp. 9⅜ x 12¼. 25124-1

Beethoven, Ludwig van, COMPLETE PIANO CONCERTOS IN FULL SCORE. Complete scores of five great Beethoven piano concertos, with all cadenzas as he wrote them, reproduced from authoritative Breitkopf & Härtel edition. New Table of Contents. 384pp. 9⅜ x 12¼. 24563-2

Beethoven, Ludwig van, SIX GREAT OVERTURES IN FULL SCORE. Six staples of the orchestral repertoire from authoritative Breitkopf & Härtel edition. *Leonore Overtures,* Nos. 1–3; Overtures to *Coriolanus, Egmont, Fidelio.* 288pp. 9 x 12. 24789-9

Beethoven, Ludwig van, SYMPHONIES NOS. 1, 2, 3, AND 4 IN FULL SCORE. Republication of H. Litolff edition. 272pp. 9 x 12. 26033-X

Beethoven, Ludwig van, SYMPHONIES NOS. 5, 6 AND 7 IN FULL SCORE, Ludwig van Beethoven. Republication of H. Litolff edition. 272pp. 9 x 12. 26034-8

Beethoven, Ludwig van, SYMPHONIES NOS. 8 AND 9 IN FULL SCORE. Republication of H. Litolff edition. 256pp. 9 x 12. 26035-6

Beethoven, Ludwig van; Mendelssohn, Felix; and Tchaikovsky, Peter Ilyitch, GREAT ROMANTIC VIOLIN CONCERTI IN FULL SCORE. The Beethoven Op. 61, Mendelssohn Op. 64 and Tchaikovsky Op. 35 concertos reprinted from Breitkopf & Härtel editions. 224pp. 9 x 12. 24989-1

Brahms, Johannes, COMPLETE CONCERTI IN FULL SCORE. Piano Concertos Nos. 1 and 2; Violin Concerto, Op. 77; Concerto for Violin and Cello, Op. 102. Definitive Breitkopf & Härtel edition. 352pp. 9⅜ x 12¼. 24170-X

Brahms, Johannes, COMPLETE SYMPHONIES. Full orchestral scores in one volume. No. 1 in C Minor, Op. 68; No. 2 in D Major, Op. 73; No. 3 in F Major, Op. 90; and No. 4 in E Minor, Op. 98. Reproduced from definitive Vienna Gesellschaft der Musikfreunde edition. Study score. 344pp. 9 x 12. 23053-8

Brahms, Johannes, THREE ORCHESTRAL WORKS IN FULL SCORE: Academic Festival Overture, Tragic Overture and Variations on a Theme by Joseph Haydn. Reproduced from the authoritative Breitkopf & Härtel edition three of Brahms's great orchestral favorites. Editor's commentary in German and English. 112pp. 9⅜ x 12¼. 24637-X

Chopin, Frédéric, THE PIANO CONCERTOS IN FULL SCORE. The authoritative Breitkopf & Härtel full-score edition in one volume; Piano Concertos No. 1 in E Minor and No. 2 in F Minor. 176pp. 9 x 12. 25835-1

Corelli, Arcangelo, COMPLETE CONCERTI GROSSI IN FULL SCORE. All 12 concerti in the famous late nineteenth-century edition prepared by violinist Joseph Joachim and musicologist Friedrich Chrysander. 240pp. 8⅜ x 11¼. 25606-5

Debussy, Claude, THREE GREAT ORCHESTRAL WORKS IN FULL SCORE. Three of the Impressionist's most-recorded, most-performed favorites: *Prélude à l'Après-midi d'un Faune, Nocturnes,* and *La Mer.* Reprinted from early French editions. 279pp. 9 x 12. 24441-5

Dvořák, Antonín, SERENADE NO. 1, OP. 22, AND SERENADE NO. 2, OP. 44, IN FULL SCORE. Two works typified by elegance of form, intense harmony, rhythmic variety, and uninhibited emotionalism. 96pp. 9 x 12. 41895-2

Dvořák, Antonín, SYMPHONY NO. 8 IN G MAJOR, OP. 88, SYMPHONY NO. 9 IN E MINOR, OP. 95 ("NEW WORLD") IN FULL SCORE. Two celebrated symphonies by the great Czech composer, the Eighth and the immensely popular Ninth, "From the New World," in one volume. 272pp. 9 x 12. 24749-X

Elgar, Edward, CELLO CONCERTO IN E MINOR, OP. 85, IN FULL SCORE. A tour de force for any cellist, this frequently performed work is widely regarded as an elegy for a lost world. Melodic and evocative, it exhibits a remarkable scope, ranging from tragic passion to buoyant optimism. Reproduced from an authoritative source. 112pp. 8⅜ x 11. 41896-0

Franck, César, SYMPHONY IN D MINOR IN FULL SCORE. Superb, authoritative edition of Franck's only symphony, an often-performed and recorded masterwork of late French romantic style. 160pp. 9 x 12. 25373-2

Handel, George Frideric, COMPLETE CONCERTI GROSSI IN FULL SCORE. Monumental Opus 6 Concerti Grossi, Opus 3 and "Alexander's Feast" Concerti Grossi–19 in all–reproduced from the most authoritative edition. 258pp. 9⅜ x 12¼. 24187-4

Handel, George Frideric, GREAT ORGAN CONCERTI, OPP. 4 & 7, IN FULL SCORE. 12 organ concerti composed by the great Baroque master are reproduced in full score from the Deutsche Handelgesellschaft edition. 138pp. 9⅜ x 12¼. 24462-8

Handel, George Frideric, WATER MUSIC AND MUSIC FOR THE ROYAL FIREWORKS IN FULL SCORE. Full scores of two of the most popular Baroque orchestral works performed today–reprinted from the definitive Deutsche Handelgesellschaft edition. Total of 96pp. 8⅛ x 11. 25070-9

Haydn, Joseph, SYMPHONIES 88–92 IN FULL SCORE: The Haydn Society Edition. Full score of symphonies Nos. 88 through 92. Large, readable noteheads, ample margins for fingerings, etc., and extensive Editor's Commentary. 304pp. 9 x 12. (Available in U.S. only) 24445-8

Liszt, Franz, THE PIANO CONCERTI IN FULL SCORE. Here in one volume are Piano Concerto No. 1 in E-flat Major and Piano Concerto No. 2 in A Major–among the most studied, recorded, and performed of all works for piano and orchestra. 144pp. 9 x 12. 25221-3

Mahler, Gustav, DAS LIED VON DER ERDE IN FULL SCORE. Mahler's masterpiece, a fusion of song and symphony, reprinted from the original 1912 Universal Edition. English translations of song texts. 160pp. 9 x 12. 25657-X

Mahler, Gustav, SYMPHONIES NOS. 1 AND 2 IN FULL SCORE. Unabridged, authoritative Austrian editions of Symphony No. 1 in D Major ("Titan") and Symphony No. 2 in C Minor ("Resurrection"). 384pp. 8⅛ x 11. 25473-9

Mahler, Gustav, SYMPHONIES NOS. 3 AND 4 IN FULL SCORE. Two brilliantly contrasting masterworks–one scored for a massive ensemble, the other for small orchestra and soloist–reprinted from authoritative Viennese editions. 368pp. 9⅜ x 12¼. 26166-2

*Available from your music dealer or write for **free** Music Catalog to*
Dover Publications, Inc., Dept. MUBI, 31 East 2nd Street, Mineola, NY 11501
*Visit us online at **www.doverpublications.com***

Dover Orchestral Scores

Mahler, Gustav, SYMPHONY NO. 8 IN FULL SCORE. Authoritative edition of massive, complex "Symphony of a Thousand." Scored for orchestra, eight solo voices, double chorus, boys' choir and organ. Reprint of Izdatel'stvo "Muzyka," Moscow, edition. Translation of texts. 272pp. 9⅜ x 12¼. 26022-4

Mendelssohn, Felix, MAJOR ORCHESTRAL WORKS IN FULL SCORE. Considered to be Mendelssohn's finest orchestral works, here in one volume are the complete *Midsummer Night's Dream; Hebrides Overture; Calm Sea and Prosperous Voyage Overture;* Symphony No. 3 in A ("Scottish"); and Symphony No. 4 in A ("Italian"). Breitkopf & Härtel edition. Study score. 406pp. 9 x 12. 23184-4

Mozart, Wolfgang Amadeus, CONCERTI FOR WIND INSTRUMENTS IN FULL SCORE. Exceptional volume contains ten pieces for orchestra and wind instruments and includes some of Mozart's finest, most popular music. 272pp. 9⅜ x 12¼. 25228-0

Mozart, Wolfgang Amadeus, LATER SYMPHONIES. Full orchestral scores to last symphonies (Nos. 35–41) reproduced from definitive Breitkopf & Härtel Complete Works edition. Study score. 285pp. 9 x 12. 23052-X

Mozart, Wolfgang Amadeus, PIANO CONCERTOS NOS. 11–16 IN FULL SCORE. Authoritative Breitkopf & Härtel edition of six staples of the concerto repertoire, including Mozart's cadenzas for Nos. 12–16. 256pp. 9⅜ x 12¼. 25468-2

Mozart, Wolfgang Amadeus, PIANO CONCERTOS NOS. 17–22 IN FULL SCORE. Six complete piano concertos in full score, with Mozart's own cadenzas for Nos. 17–19. Breitkopf & Härtel edition. Study score. 370pp. 9⅜ x 12¼. 23599-8

Mozart, Wolfgang Amadeus, PIANO CONCERTOS NOS. 23–27 IN FULL SCORE. Mozart's last five piano concertos in full score, plus cadenzas for Nos. 23 and 27, and the Concert Rondo in D Major, K.382. Breitkopf & Härtel edition. Study score. 310pp. 9⅜ x 12¼. 23600-5

Mozart, Wolfgang Amadeus, 17 DIVERTIMENTI FOR VARIOUS INSTRUMENTS. Sparkling pieces of great vitality and brilliance from 1771 to 1779; consecutively numbered from 1 to 17. Reproduced from definitive Breitkopf & Härtel Complete Works edition. Study score. 241pp. 9⅜ x 12¼. 23862-8

Mozart, Wolfgang Amadeus, THE VIOLIN CONCERTI AND THE SINFONIA CONCERTANTE, K.364, IN FULL SCORE. All five violin concerti and famed double concerto reproduced from authoritative Breitkopf & Härtel Complete Works Edition. 208pp. 9⅜ x 12¼. 25169-1

Ravel, Maurice, DAPHNIS AND CHLOE IN FULL SCORE. Definitive full-score edition of Ravel's rich musical setting of a Greek fable by Longus is reprinted here from the original French edition. 320pp. 9⅜ x 12¼. (Not available in France or Germany) 25826-2

Ravel, Maurice, LE TOMBEAU DE COUPERIN and VALSES NOBLES ET SENTIMENTALES IN FULL SCORE. *Le Tombeau de Couperin* consists of "Prelude," "Forlane," "Menuet," and "Rigaudon"; the uninterrupted 8 waltzes of *Valses Nobles et Sentimentales* abound with lilting rhythms and unexpected harmonic subtleties. 144pp. 9⅜ x 12¼. (Not available in France or Germany) 41898-7

Ravel, Maurice, RAPSODIE ESPAGNOLE, MOTHER GOOSE and PAVANE FOR A DEAD PRINCESS IN FULL SCORE. Full authoritative scores of 3 enormously popular works by the great French composer, each rich in orchestral settings. 160pp. 9⅜ x 12¼. 41899-5

Schubert, Franz, FOUR SYMPHONIES IN FULL SCORE. Schubert's four most popular symphonies: No. 4 in C Minor ("Tragic"); No. 5 in B-flat Major; No. 8 in B Minor ("Unfinished"); and No. 9 in C Major ("Great"). Breitkopf & Härtel edition. Study score. 261pp. 9⅜ x 12¼. 23681-1

Schubert, Franz, SYMPHONY NO. 3 IN D MAJOR AND SYMPHONY NO. 6 IN C MAJOR IN FULL SCORE. The former is scored for 12 wind instruments and timpani; the latter is known as "The Little Symphony in C" to distinguish it from Symphony No. 9, "The Great Symphony in C." Authoritative editions. 128pp. 9⅜ x 12¼. 42134-1

Schumann, Robert, COMPLETE SYMPHONIES IN FULL SCORE. No. 1 in B-flat Major, Op. 38 ("Spring"); No. 2 in C Major, Op. 61; No. 3 in E-flat Major, Op. 97 ("Rhenish"); and No. 4 in D Minor, Op. 120. Breitkopf & Härtel editions. Study score. 416pp. 9⅜ x 12¼. 24013-4

Schumann, Robert, GREAT WORKS FOR PIANO AND ORCHESTRA IN FULL SCORE. Collection of three superb pieces for piano and orchestra, including the popular Piano Concerto in A Minor. Breitkopf & Härtel edition. 183pp. 9⅜ x 12¼. 24340-0

Strauss, Johann, Jr., THE GREAT WALTZES IN FULL SCORE. Complete scores of eight melodic masterpieces: "The Beautiful Blue Danube," "Emperor Waltz," "Tales of the Vienna Woods," "Wiener Blut," and four more. Authoritative editions. 336pp. 8⅜ x 11¼. 26009-7

Strauss, Richard, TONE POEMS, SERIES I: DON JUAN, TOD UND VERKLARUNG, and DON QUIXOTE IN FULL SCORE. Three of the most often performed and recorded works in entire orchestral repertoire, reproduced in full score from original editions. 286pp. 9⅜ x 12¼. (Available in U.S. only) 23754-0

Strauss, Richard, TONE POEMS, SERIES II: TILL EULENSPIEGELS LUSTIGE STREICHE, "ALSO SPRACH ZARATHUSTRA," and EIN HELDENLEBEN IN FULL SCORE. Three important orchestral works, including very popular *Till Eulenspiegel's Merry Pranks,* reproduced in full score from original editions. Study score. 315pp. 9⅜ x 12¼. (Available in U.S. only) 23755-9

Stravinsky, Igor, THE FIREBIRD IN FULL SCORE (Original 1910 Version). Inexpensive edition of modern masterpiece, renowned for brilliant orchestration, glowing color. Authoritative Russian edition. 176pp. 9⅜ x 12¼. (Available in U.S. only) 25535-2

Stravinsky, Igor, PETRUSHKA IN FULL SCORE: Original Version. Full-score edition of Stravinsky's masterful score for the great Ballets Russes 1911 production of *Petrushka.* 160pp. 9⅜ x 12¼. (Available in U.S. only) 25680-4

Stravinsky, Igor, THE RITE OF SPRING IN FULL SCORE. Full-score edition of most famous musical work of the 20th century, created as a ballet score for Diaghilev's Ballets Russes. 176pp. 9⅜ x 12¼. (Available in U.S. only) 25857-2

Tchaikovsky, Peter Ilyitch, FOURTH, FIFTH AND SIXTH SYMPHONIES IN FULL SCORE. Complete orchestral scores of Symphony No. 4 in F Minor, Op. 36; Symphony No. 5 in E Minor, Op. 64; Symphony No. 6 in B Minor, "Pathetique," Op. 74. Study score. Breitkopf & Härtel editions. 480pp. 9⅜ x 12¼. 23861-X

Tchaikovsky, Peter Ilyitch, NUTCRACKER SUITE IN FULL SCORE. Among the most popular ballet pieces ever created; available in a complete, inexpensive, high-quality score to study and enjoy. 128pp. 9 x 12. 25379-1

Tchaikovsky, Peter Ilyitch, ROMEO AND JULIET OVERTURE AND CAPRICCIO ITALIEN IN FULL SCORE. Two of Russian master's most popular compositions. From authoritative Russian edition; new translation of Russian footnotes. 208pp. 8⅜ x 11¼. 25217-5

von Weber, Carl Maria, GREAT OVERTURES IN FULL SCORE. Overtures to *Oberon, Der Freischutz, Euryanthe* and *Preciosa* reprinted from authoritative Breitkopf & Härtel editions. 112pp. 9 x 12. 25225-6

*Available from your music dealer or write for **free** Music Catalog to*
Dover Publications, Inc., Dept. MUBI, 31 East 2nd Street, Mineola, NY 11501
*Visit us online at **www.doverpublications.com***

Dover Piano and Keyboard Editions

Albeniz, Isaac, IBERIA AND ESPAÑA: Two Complete Works for Solo Piano. Spanish composer's greatest piano works in authoritative editions. Includes the popular "Tango." 192pp. 9 x 12. 25367-8

Bach, Carl Philipp Emanuel, GREAT KEYBOARD SONATAS. Comprehensive two-volume edition contains 51 sonatas by second, most prestigious son of Johann Sebastian Bach. Originality, rich harmony, delicate workmanship. Authoritative French edition. Total of 384pp. 8⅜ x 11¼.
Series I 24853-4
Series II 24854-2

Bach, Johann Sebastian, COMPLETE KEYBOARD TRANSCRIPTIONS OF CONCERTOS BY BAROQUE COMPOSERS. Sixteen concertos by Vivaldi, Telemann and others, transcribed for solo keyboard instruments. Bach-Gesellschaft edition. 128pp. 9⅜ x 12¼. 25529-8

Bach, Johann Sebastian, COMPLETE PRELUDES AND FUGUES FOR ORGAN. All 25 of Bach's complete sets of preludes and fugues (i.e. compositions written as pairs), from the authoritative Bach-Gesellschaft edition. 168pp. 8⅜ x 11. 24816-X

Bach, Johann Sebastian, ITALIAN CONCERTO, CHROMATIC FANTASIA AND FUGUE AND OTHER WORKS FOR KEYBOARD. Sixteen of Bach's best-known, most-performed and most-recorded works for the keyboard, reproduced from the authoritative Bach-Gesellschaft edition. 112pp. 9 x 12. 25387-2

Bach, Johann Sebastian, KEYBOARD MUSIC. Bach-Gesellschaft edition. For harpsichord, piano, other keyboard instruments. English Suites, French Suites, Six Partitas, Goldberg Variations, Two-Part Inventions, Three-Part Sinfonias. 312pp. 8⅛ x 11. 22360-4

Bach, Johann Sebastian, ORGAN MUSIC. Bach-Gesellschaft edition. 93 works. 6 Trio Sonatas, German Organ Mass, Orgelbüchlein, Six Schubler Chorales, 18 Choral Preludes. 357pp. 8⅛ x 11. 22359-0

Bach, Johann Sebastian, TOCCATAS, FANTASIAS, PASSACAGLIA AND OTHER WORKS FOR ORGAN. Over 20 best-loved works including Toccata and Fugue in D Minor, BWV 565; Passacaglia and Fugue in C Minor, BWV 582, many more. Bach-Gesellschaft edition. 176pp. 9 x 12. 25403-8

Bach, Johann Sebastian, TWO- AND THREE-PART INVENTIONS. Reproduction of original autograph ms. Edited by Eric Simon. 62pp. 8⅛ x 11. 21982-8

Bach, Johann Sebastian, THE WELL-TEMPERED CLAVIER: Books I and II, Complete. All 48 preludes and fugues in all major and minor keys. Authoritative Bach-Gesellschaft edition. Explanation of ornaments in English, tempo indications, music corrections. 208pp. 9⅜ x 12¼. 24532-2

Bartók, Béla, PIANO MUSIC OF BÉLA BARTÓK, Series I. New, definitive Archive Edition incorporating composer's corrections. Includes *Funeral March* from Kossuth, *Fourteen Bagatelles*, Bartók's break to modernism. 167pp. 9 x 12. (Available in U.S. only) 24108-4

Bartók, Béla, PIANO MUSIC OF BÉLA BARTÓK, Series II. Second in the Archive Edition incorporating composer's corrections. 85 short pieces *For Children, Two Elegies, Two Romanian Dances,* etc. 192pp. 9 x 12. (Available in U.S. only) 24109-2

Beethoven, Ludwig van, BAGATELLES, RONDOS AND OTHER SHORTER WORKS FOR PIANO. Most popular and most performed shorter works, including Rondo a capriccio in G and Andante in F. Breitkopf & Härtel edition. 128pp. 9⅜ x 12¼. 25392-9

Beethoven, Ludwig van, COMPLETE PIANO SONATAS. All sonatas in fine Schenker edition, with fingering, analytical material. One of best modern editions. 615pp. 9 x 12. Two-vol. set. 23134-8, 23135-6

Beethoven, Ludwig van, COMPLETE VARIATIONS FOR SOLO PIANO, Ludwig van Beethoven. Contains all 21 sets of Beethoven's piano variations, including the extremely popular *Diabelli Variations, Op. 120.* 240pp. 9⅜ x 12¼. 25188-8

Blesh, Rudi (ed.), CLASSIC PIANO RAGS. Best ragtime music (1897–1922) by Scott Joplin, James Scott, Joseph F. Lamb, Tom Turpin, nine others. 364pp. 9 x 12. Introduction by Blesh. 20469-3

Brahms, Johannes, COMPLETE SHORTER WORKS FOR SOLO PIANO. All solo music not in other two volumes. Waltzes, Scherzo in E Flat Minor, Eight Pieces, Rhapsodies, Fantasies, Intermezzi, etc. Vienna Gesellschaft der Musikfreunde. 180pp. 9 x 12. 22651-4

Brahms, Johannes, COMPLETE SONATAS AND VARIATIONS FOR SOLO PIANO. All sonatas, five variations on themes from Schumann, Paganini, Handel, etc. Vienna Gesellschaft der Musikfreunde edition. 178pp. 9 x 12. 22650-6

Brahms, Johannes, COMPLETE TRANSCRIPTIONS, CADENZAS AND EXERCISES FOR SOLO PIANO. Vienna Gesellschaft der Musikfreunde edition, vol. 15. Studies after Chopin, Weber, Bach; gigues, sarabandes; 10 Hungarian dances, etc. 178pp. 9 x 12. 22652-2

Buxtehude, Dietrich, ORGAN WORKS. Complete organ works of extremely influential pre-Bach composer. Toccatas, preludes, chorales, more. Definitive Breitkopf & Härtel edition. 320pp. 8⅜ x 11¼. (Available in U.S. only) 25682-0

Byrd, William, MY LADY NEVELLS BOOKE OF VIRGINAL MUSIC. 42 compositions in modern notation from 1591 ms. For any keyboard instrument. 245pp. 8⅛ x 11. 22246-2

Chopin, Frédéric, COMPLETE BALLADES, IMPROMPTUS AND SONATAS. The four Ballades, four Impromptus and three Sonatas. Authoritative Mikuli edition. 192pp. 9 x 12. 24164-5

Chopin, Frédéric, COMPLETE MAZURKAS, Frédéric Chopin. 51 best-loved compositions, reproduced directly from the authoritative Kistner edition edited by Carl Mikuli. 160pp. 9 x 12. 25548-4

Chopin, Frédéric, COMPLETE PRELUDES AND ETUDES FOR SOLO PIANO. All 25 Preludes and all 27 Etudes by greatest piano music composer. Authoritative Mikuli edition. 192pp. 9 x 12. 24052-5

Chopin, Frédéric, FANTASY IN F MINOR, BARCAROLLE, BERCEUSE AND OTHER WORKS FOR SOLO PIANO. 15 works, including one of the greatest of the Romantic period, the Fantasy in F Minor, Op. 49, reprinted from the authoritative German edition prepared by Chopin's student, Carl Mikuli. 224pp. 8⅜ x 11¼. 25950-1

Chopin, Frédéric, NOCTURNES AND POLONAISES. 20 *Nocturnes* and 11 *Polonaises* reproduced from the authoritative Mikuli edition for pianists, students, and musicologists. Commentary. 224pp. 9 x 12. 24564-0

Chopin, Frédéric, WALTZES AND SCHERZOS. All of the Scherzos and nearly all (20) of the Waltzes from the authoritative Mikuli edition. Editorial commentary. 160pp. 9 x 12. 24316-8

Cofone, Charles J. F. (ed.), ELIZABETH ROGERS HIR VIRGINALL BOOKE. All 112 pieces from noted 1656 manuscript, most never before published. Composers include Thomas Brewer, William Byrd, Orlando Gibbons, etc. Calligraphy by editor. 125pp. 9 x 12. 23138-0

Available from your music dealer or write for free Music Catalog to
Dover Publications, Inc., Dept. MUBI, 31 East 2nd Street, Mineola, NY 11501
Visit us online at www.doverpublications.com

Dover Piano and Keyboard Editions

Couperin, François, KEYBOARD WORKS/Series One: Ordres I–XIII; Series Two: Ordres XIV–XXVII and Miscellaneous Pieces. Over 200 pieces. Reproduced directly from edition prepared by Johannes Brahms and Friedrich Chrysander. Total of 496pp. 8⅛ x 11. Series I 25795-9 Series II 25796-7

Debussy, Claude, COMPLETE PRELUDES, Books 1 and 2. 24 evocative works that reveal the essence of Debussy's genius for musical imagery, among them many of the composer's most famous piano compositions. Glossary of French terms. 128pp. 8⅜ x 11¼. 25970-6

Debussy, Claude, DEBUSSY MASTERPIECES FOR SOLO PIANO: 20 Works. From France's most innovative and influential composer–a rich compilation of works that include "Golliwogg's cakewalk," "Engulfed cathedral," "Clair de lune," and 17 others. 128pp. 9 x 12. 42425-1

Debussy, Claude, PIANO MUSIC 1888–1905. Deux Arabesques, Suite Bergamesque, Masques, first series of Images, etc. Nine others, in corrected editions. 175pp. 9⅜ x 12¼. 22771-5

Dvořák, Antonín, HUMORESQUES AND OTHER WORKS FOR SOLO PIANO. Humoresques, Op. 101, complete, Silhouettes, Op. 8, Poetic Tone Pictures, Theme with Variations, Op. 36, 4 Slavonic Dances, more. 160pp. 9 x 12. 28355-0

Fauré, Gabriel, COMPLETE PRELUDES, IMPROMPTUS AND VALSES-CAPRICES. Eighteen elegantly wrought piano works in authoritative editions. Only one-volume collection available. 144pp. 9 x 12. (Not available in France or Germany) 25789-4

Fauré, Gabriel, NOCTURNES AND BARCAROLLES FOR SOLO PIANO. 12 nocturnes and 12 barcarolles reprinted from authoritative French editions. 208pp. 9⅜ x 12¼. (Not available in France or Germany) 27955-3

Feofanov, Dmitry (ed.), RARE MASTERPIECES OF RUSSIAN PIANO MUSIC: Eleven Pieces by Glinka, Balakirev, Glazunov and Others. Glinka's *Prayer,* Balakirev's *Reverie,* Liapunov's *Transcendental Etude, Op. 11, No. 10,* and eight others–full, authoritative scores from Russian texts. 144pp. 9 x 12. 24659-0

Franck, César, ORGAN WORKS. Composer's best-known works for organ, including Six Pieces, Trois Pieces, and Trois Chorals. Oblong format for easy use at keyboard. Authoritative Durand edition. 208pp. 11⅜ x 8¼. 25517-4

Franck, César, SELECTED PIANO COMPOSITIONS, edited by Vincent d'Indy. Outstanding selection of influential French composer's piano works, including early pieces and the two masterpieces–Prelude, Choral and Fugue; and Prelude, Aria and Finale. Ten works in all. 138pp. 9 x 12. 23269-7

Gillespie, John (ed.), NINETEENTH-CENTURY EUROPEAN PIANO MUSIC: Unfamiliar Masterworks. Difficult-to-find etudes, toccatas, polkas, impromptus, waltzes, etc., by Albéniz, Bizet, Chabrier, Fauré, Smetana, Richard Strauss, Wagner and 16 other composers. 62 pieces. 343pp. 9 x 12. (Not available in France or Germany) 23447-9

Gottschalk, Louis M., PIANO MUSIC. 26 pieces (including covers) by early 19th-century American genius. "Bamboula," "The Banjo," other Creole, Negro-based material, through elegant salon music. 301pp. 9¼ x 12. 21683-7

Granados, Enrique, GOYESCAS, SPANISH DANCES AND OTHER WORKS FOR SOLO PIANO. Great Spanish composer's most admired, most performed suites for the piano, in definitive Spanish editions. 176pp. 9 x 12. 25481-X

Grieg, Edvard, COMPLETE LYRIC PIECES FOR PIANO. All 66 pieces from Grieg's ten sets of little mood pictures for piano, favorites of generations of pianists. 224pp. 9⅜ x 12¼. 26176-X

Handel, G. F., KEYBOARD WORKS FOR SOLO INSTRUMENTS. 35 neglected works from Handel's vast oeuvre, originally jotted down as improvisations. Includes Eight Great Suites, others. New sequence. 174pp. 9⅜ x 12¼. 24338-9

Haydn, Joseph, COMPLETE PIANO SONATAS. 52 sonatas reprinted from authoritative Breitkopf & Härtel edition. Extremely clear and readable; ample space for notes, analysis. 464pp. 9⅜ x 12¼. Vol. I 24726-0 Vol. II 24727-9

Jasen, David A. (ed.), RAGTIME GEMS: Original Sheet Music for 25 Ragtime Classics. Includes original sheet music and covers for 25 rags, including three of Scott Joplin's finest: "Searchlight Rag," "Rose Leaf Rag," and "Fig Leaf Rag." 122pp. 9 x 12. 25248-5

Joplin, Scott, COMPLETE PIANO RAGS. All 38 piano rags by the acknowledged master of the form, reprinted from the publisher's original editions complete with sheet music covers. Introduction by David A. Jasen. 208pp. 9 x 12. 25807-6

Liszt, Franz, ANNÉES DE PÈLERINAGE, COMPLETE. Authoritative Russian edition of piano masterpieces: *Première Année (Suisse): Deuxième Année (Italie)* and *Venezia e Napoli; Troisième Année,* other related pieces. 288pp. 9⅜ x 12¼. 25627-8

Liszt, Franz, BEETHOVEN SYMPHONIES NOS. 6–9 TRANSCRIBED FOR SOLO PIANO. Includes Symphony No. 6 in F major, Op. 68, "Pastorale"; Symphony No. 7 in A major, Op. 92; Symphony No. 8 in F major, Op. 93; and Symphony No. 9 in D minor, Op. 125, "Choral." A memorable tribute from one musical genius to another. 224pp. 9 x 12. 41884-7

Liszt, Franz, COMPLETE ETUDES FOR SOLO PIANO, Series I: Including the Transcendental Etudes, edited by Busoni. Also includes Etude in 12 Exercises, 12 Grandes Etudes and Mazeppa. Breitkopf & Härtel edition. 272pp. 8⅜ x 11¼. 25815-7

Liszt, Franz, COMPLETE ETUDES FOR SOLO PIANO, Series II: Including the Paganini Etudes and Concert Etudes, edited by Busoni. Also includes Morceau de Salon, Ab Irato. Breitkopf & Härtel edition. 192pp. 8⅜ x 11¼. 25816-5

Liszt, Franz, COMPLETE HUNGARIAN RHAPSODIES FOR SOLO PIANO. All 19 Rhapsodies reproduced directly from authoritative Russian edition. All headings, footnotes translated to English. 224pp. 8⅜ x 11¼. 24744-9

Liszt, Franz, MEPHISTO WALTZ AND OTHER WORKS FOR SOLO PIANO. Rapsodie Espagnole, Liebestraüme Nos. 1–3, Valse Oubliée No. 1, Nuages Gris, Polonaises Nos. 1 and 2, Grand Galop Chromatique, more. 192pp. 8⅜ x 11¼. 28147-7

Liszt, Franz, PIANO TRANSCRIPTIONS FROM FRENCH AND ITALIAN OPERAS. Virtuoso transformations of themes by Mozart, Verdi, Bellini, other masters, into unforgettable music for piano. Published in association with American Liszt Society. 247pp. 9 x 12. 24273-0

Liszt, Franz, SONATA IN B MINOR AND OTHER WORKS FOR PIANO. One of Liszt's most frequently performed piano masterpieces, with the six Consolations, ten *Harmonies poetiques et religieuses,* two Ballades and two Legendes. Breitkopf & Härtel edition. 208pp. 8⅜ x 11¼. 26182-4

Maitland, J. Fuller, Squire, W. B. (eds.), THE FITZWILLIAM VIRGINAL BOOK. Famous early 17th-century collection of keyboard music, 300 works by Morley, Byrd, Bull, Gibbons, etc. Modern notation. Total of 938pp. 8⅜ x 11. Two-vol. set. 21068-5, 21069-3

Available from your music dealer or write for ***free*** *Music Catalog to*
Dover Publications, Inc., Dept. MUBI, 31 East 2nd Street, Mineola, NY 11501
Visit us online at ***www.doverpublications.com***

Dover Piano and Keyboard Editions

Mendelssohn, Felix, COMPLETE WORKS FOR PIANOFORTE SOLO. Breitkopf and Härtel edition of Capriccio in F# Minor, Sonata in E Major, Fantasy in F# Minor, Three Caprices, Songs without Words, and 20 other works. Total of 416pp. 9⅜ x 12¼. Two-vol. set. 23136-4, 23137-2

Mozart, Wolfgang Amadeus, MOZART MASTERPIECES: 19 WORKS FOR SOLO PIANO. Superb assortment includes sonatas, fantasies, variations, rondos, minuets, and more. Highlights include "Turkish Rondo," "Sonata in C," and a dozen variations on "Ah, vous dirai-je, Maman" (the familiar tune "Twinkle, Twinkle, Little Star"). Convenient, attractive, inexpensive volume; authoritative sources. 128pp. 9 x 12. 40408-0

Pachelbel, Johann, THE FUGUES ON THE MAGNIFICAT FOR ORGAN OR KEYBOARD. 94 pieces representative of Pachelbel's magnificent contribution to keyboard composition; can be played on the organ, harpsichord or piano. 100pp. 9 x 12. (Available in U.S. only) 25037-7

Phillipp, Isidor (ed.), FRENCH PIANO MUSIC, AN ANTHOLOGY. 44 complete works, 1670–1905, by Lully, Couperin, Rameau, Alkan, Saint-Saëns, Delibes, Bizet, Godard, many others; favorite and lesser-known examples, all top quality. 188pp. 9 x 12. (Not available in France or Germany) 23381-2

Prokofiev, Sergei, PIANO SONATAS NOS. 1–4, OPP. 1, 14, 28, 29. Includes the dramatic Sonata No. 1 in F minor; Sonata No. 2 in D minor, a masterpiece in four movements; Sonata No. 3 in A minor, a brilliant 7-minute score; and Sonata No. 4 in C minor, a three-movement sonata considered vintage Prokofiev. 96pp. 9 x 12. (Available in U.S. only) 42128-7

Rachmaninoff, Serge, COMPLETE PRELUDES AND ETUDES-TABLEAUX. Forty-one of his greatest works for solo piano, including the riveting C Minor, G Minor and B Minor preludes, in authoritative editions. 208pp. 8⅜ x 11¼. 25696-0

Ravel, Maurice, PIANO MASTERPIECES OF MAURICE RAVEL. Handsome affordable treasury; *Pavane pour une infante defunte, jeux d'eau, Sonatine, Miroirs,* more. 128pp. 9 x 12. (Not available in France or Germany) 25137-3

Satie, Erik, GYMNOPÉDIES, GNOSSIENNES AND OTHER WORKS FOR PIANO. The largest Satie collection of piano works yet published, 17 in all, reprinted from the original French editions. 176pp. 9 x 12. (Not available in France or Germany) 25978-1

Satie, Erik, TWENTY SHORT PIECES FOR PIANO (Sports et Divertissements). French master's brilliant thumbnail sketches–verbal and musical–of various outdoor sports and amusements. English translations, 20 illustrations. Rare, limited 1925 edition. 48pp. 12 x 8⅞. (Not available in France or Germany) 24365-6

Scarlatti, Domenico, GREAT KEYBOARD SONATAS, Series I and Series II. 78 of the most popular sonatas reproduced from the G. Ricordi edition edited by Alessandro Longo. Total of 320pp. 8⅜ x 11¼.
Series I 24996-4
Series II 25003-2

Schubert, Franz, COMPLETE SONATAS FOR PIANOFORTE SOLO. All 15 sonatas. Breitkopf and Härtel edition. 293pp. 9⅜ x 12¼. 22647-6

Schubert, Franz, DANCES FOR SOLO PIANO. Over 350 waltzes, minuets, landler, ecossaises, and other charming, melodic dance compositions reprinted from the authoritative Breitkopf & Härtel edition. 192pp. 9⅜ x 12¼. 26107-7

Schubert, Franz, SELECTED PIANO WORKS FOR FOUR HANDS. 24 separate pieces (16 most popular titles): Three Military Marches, Lebensstürme, Four Polonaises, Four Ländler, etc. Rehearsal numbers added. 273pp. 9 x 12. 23529-7

Schubert, Franz, SHORTER WORKS FOR PIANOFORTE SOLO. All piano music except Sonatas, Dances, and a few unfinished pieces. Contains Wanderer, Impromptus, Moments Musicals, Variations, Scherzi, etc. Breitkopf and Härtel edition. 199pp. 9⅜ x 12¼. 22648-4

Schumann, Clara (ed.), PIANO MUSIC OF ROBERT SCHUMANN, Series I. Major compositions from the period 1830–39; *Papillons,* Toccata, Grosse Sonate No. 1, *Phantasiestücke, Arabeske, Blumenstück,* and nine other works. Reprinted from Breitkopf & Härtel edition. 274pp. 9⅜ x 12¼. 21459-1

Schumann, Clara (ed.), PIANO MUSIC OF ROBERT SCHUMANN, Series II. Major compositions from period 1838–53; *Humoreske, Novelletten,* Sonate No. 2, 43 *Clavierstücke für die Jugend,* and six other works. Reprinted from Breitkopf & Härtel edition. 272pp. 9⅜ x 12¼. 21461-3

Schumann, Clara (ed.), PIANO MUSIC OF ROBERT SCHUMANN, Series III. All solo music not in other two volumes, including *Symphonic Etudes, Phantaisie,* 13 other choice works. Definitive Breitkopf & Härtel edition. 224pp. 9⅜ x 12¼. 23906-3

Scriabin, Alexander, COMPLETE PIANO SONATAS. All ten of Scriabin's sonatas, reprinted from an authoritative early Russian edition. 256pp. 8⅜ x 11¼. 25850-5

Scriabin, Alexander, THE COMPLETE PRELUDES AND ETUDES FOR PIANOFORTE SOLO. All the preludes and etudes including many perfectly spun miniatures. Edited by K. N. Igumnov and Y. I. Mil'shteyn. 250pp. 9 x 12. 22919-X

Sousa, John Philip, SOUSA'S GREAT MARCHES IN PIANO TRANSCRIPTION. Playing edition includes: "The Stars and Stripes Forever," "King Cotton," "Washington Post," much more. 24 illustrations. 111pp. 9 x 12. 23132-1

Strauss, Johann, Jr., FAVORITE WALTZES, POLKAS AND OTHER DANCES FOR SOLO PIANO. "Blue Danube," "Tales from Vienna Woods," and many other best-known waltzes and other dances. 160pp. 9 x 12. 27851-4

Sweelinck, Jan Pieterszoon, WORKS FOR ORGAN AND KEYBOARD. Nearly all of early Dutch composer's difficult-to-find keyboard works. Chorale variations; toccatas, fantasias; variations on secular, dance tunes. Also, incomplete and/or modified works, plus fantasia by John Bull. 272pp. 9 x 12. 24935-2

Telemann, Georg Philipp, THE 36 FANTASIAS FOR KEYBOARD. Graceful compositions by 18th-century master. 1923 Breslauer edition. 80pp. 8⅛ x 11. 25365-1

Tichenor, Trebor Jay, (ed.), RAGTIME RARITIES. 63 tuneful, rediscovered piano rags by 51 composers (or teams). Does not duplicate selections in *Classic Piano Rags* (Dover, 20469-3). 305pp. 9 x 12. 23157-7

Tichenor, Trebor Jay, (ed.), RAGTIME REDISCOVERIES. 64 unusual rags demonstrate diversity of style, local tradition. Original sheet music. 320pp. 9 x 12. 23776-1

*Available from your music dealer or write for **free** Music Catalog to*
Dover Publications, Inc., Dept. MUBI, 31 East 2nd Street, Mineola, NY 11501
*Visit us online at **www.doverpublications.com***

Dover Popular Songbooks

(Arranged by title)

ALEXANDER'S RAGTIME BAND AND OTHER FAVORITE SONG HITS, 1901–1911, David A. Jasen (ed.). Fifty vintage popular songs America still sings, reprinted in their entirety from the original editions. Introduction. 224pp. 9 x 12. (Available in U.S. only)   25331-7

AMERICAN BALLADS AND FOLK SONGS, John A. Lomax and Alan Lomax. Over 200 songs, music and lyrics: "Frankie and Albert," "John Henry," "Frog Went a-Courtin'," "Down in the Valley," "Skip to My Lou," other favorites. Notes on each song. 672pp. 5⅜ x 8½.   28276-7

AMERICAN FOLK SONGS FOR GUITAR, David Nadal (ed.). Forty-nine classics for beginning and intermediate guitar players, including "Beautiful Dreamer," "Amazing Grace," "Aura Lee," "John Henry," "The Gift to Be Simple," "Go Down, Moses," "Sweet Betsy from Pike," "Short'nin Bread," many more. 96pp. 9 x 12.   41700-X

THE AMERICAN SONG TREASURY: 100 Favorites, Theodore Raph (ed.). Complete piano arrangements, guitar chords, and lyrics for 100 best-loved tunes, "Buffalo Gals," "Oh, Suzanna," "Clementine," "Camptown Races," and much more. 416pp. 8⅜ x 11.   25222-1

"BEALE STREET" AND OTHER CLASSIC BLUES: 38 Works, 1901–1921, David A. Jasen (ed.). "St. Louis Blues," "The Hesitating Blues," "Down Home Blues," "Jelly Roll Blues," "Railroad Blues," and many more. Reproduced directly from rare sheet music (including original covers). Introduction. 160pp. 9 x 12. (Available in U.S. only)   40183-9

THE CIVIL WAR SONGBOOK, Richard Crawford (ed.). 37 songs: "Battle Hymn of the Republic," "Drummer Boy of Shiloh," "Dixie," and 34 more. 157pp. 9 x 12.   23422-3

CIVIL WAR SONGS AND BALLADS FOR GUITAR, Compiled, Edited, and Arranged by Jerry Silverman. 41 favorites, among them "Marching Through Georgia," "The Battle Hymn of the Republic," "Tenting on the Old Camp Ground," and "When Johnny Comes Marching Home." 160pp. 9 x 12.   41902-9

FAVORITE CHRISTMAS CAROLS, selected and arranged by Charles J. F. Cofone. Title, music, first verse and refrain of 34 traditional carols in handsome calligraphy; also subsequent verses and other information in type. 79pp. 8⅜ x 11.   20445-6

FAVORITE SONGS OF THE NINETIES, Robert Fremont (ed.). 88 favorites: "Ta-Ra-Ra-Boom-De-Aye," "The Band Played on," "Bird in a Gilded Cage," etc. 401pp. 9 x 12.   21536-9

500 BEST-LOVED SONG LYRICS, Ronald Herder (ed.). Complete lyrics for well-known folk songs, hymns, popular and show tunes, more. "Oh Susanna," "The Battle Hymn of the Republic," "When Johnny Comes Marching Home," hundreds more. Indispensable for singalongs, parties, family get-togethers, etc. 416pp. 5⅜ x 8½.   29725-X

"FOR ME AND MY GAL" AND OTHER FAVORITE SONG HITS, 1915–1917, David A. Jasen (ed.). 31 great hits: Pretty Baby, MacNamara's Band, Over There, Old Grey Mare, Beale Street, M-O-T-H-E-R, more, with original sheet music covers, complete vocal and piano. 144pp. 9 x 12.   28127-2

MY FIRST BOOK OF AMERICAN FOLK SONGS: 20 Favorite Pieces in Easy Piano Arrangements, Bergerac (ed.). Expert settings of traditional favorites by a well-known composer and arranger for young pianists: *Amazing Grace, Blue Tail Fly, Sweet Betsy from Pike,* many more. 48pp. 8¼ x 11.   28885-4

MY FIRST BOOK OF CHRISTMAS SONGS: 20 Favorite Songs in Easy Piano Arrangements, Bergerac (ed.). Beginners will love playing these beloved favorites in easy arrangements: "Jingle Bells," "Deck the Halls," "Joy to the World," "Silent Night," "Away in a Manger," "Hark! The Herald Angels Sing," 14 more. Illustrations. 48pp. 8¼ x 11.   29718-7

ONE HUNDRED ENGLISH FOLKSONGS, Cecil J. Sharp (ed.). Border ballads, folksongs, collected from all over Great Britain. "Lord Bateman," "Henry Martin," "The Green Wedding," many others. Piano. 235pp. 9 x 12.   23192-5

"PEG O' MY HEART" AND OTHER FAVORITE SONG HITS, 1912 & 1913, Stanley Appelbaum (ed.). 36 songs by Berlin, Herbert, Handy and others, with complete lyrics, full piano arrangements and original sheet music covers in black and white. 176pp. 9 x 12.   25998-6

POPULAR IRISH SONGS, Florence Leniston (ed.). 37 all-time favorites with vocal and piano arrangements: "My Wild Irish Rose," "Irish Eyes are Smiling," "Last Rose of Summer," "Danny Boy," many more. 160pp.   26755-5

"A PRETTY GIRL IS LIKE A MELODY" AND OTHER FAVORITE SONG HITS, 1918–1919, David A. Jasen (ed.). "After You've Gone," "How Ya Gonna Keep 'Em Down on the Farm," "I'm Always Chasing Rainbows," "Rock-a-Bye Your Baby" and 36 other Golden Oldies. 176pp. 9 x 12.   29421-8

A RUSSIAN SONG BOOK, Rose N. Rubin and Michael Stillman (eds.). 25 traditional folk songs, plus 19 popular songs by twentieth-century composers. Full piano arrangements, guitar chords. Lyrics in original Cyrillic, transliteration and English translation. With discography. 112pp. 9 x 12.   26118-2

"THE ST. LOUIS BLUES" AND OTHER SONG HITS OF 1914, Sandy Marrone (ed.). Full vocal and piano for "By the Beautiful Sea," "Play a Simple Melody," "They Didn't Believe Me,"–21 songs in all. 112pp. 9 x 12.   26383-5

SEVENTY SCOTTISH SONGS, Helen Hopekirk (ed.). Complete piano and vocals for classics of Scottish song: *Flow Gently, Sweet Afton, Comin' thro' the Rye (Gin a Body Meet a Body), The Campbells are Comin', Robin Adair,* many more. 208pp. 8⅜ x 11.   27029-7

SONGS OF THE CIVIL WAR, Irwin Silber (ed.). Piano, vocal, guitar chords for 125 songs including "Battle Cry of Freedom," "Marching Through Georgia," "Dixie," "Oh, I'm a Good Old Rebel," "The Drummer Boy of Shiloh," many more. 400pp. 8⅜ x 11.   28438-7

STEPHEN FOSTER SONG BOOK, Stephen Foster. 40 favorites: "Beautiful Dreamer," "Camptown Races," "Jeanie with the Light Brown Hair," "My Old Kentucky Home," etc. 224pp. 9 x 12.   23048-1

"TAKE ME OUT TO THE BALL GAME" AND OTHER FAVORITE SONG HITS, 1906–1908, Lester Levy (ed.). 23 favorite songs from the turn-of-the-century with lyrics and original sheet music covers: "Cuddle Up a Little Closer, Lovey Mine," "Harrigan," "Shine on, Harvest Moon," "School Days," other hits. 128pp. 9 x 12.   24662-0

35 SONG HITS BY GREAT BLACK SONGWRITERS: Bert Williams, Eubie Blake, Ernest Hogan and Others, David A. Jasen (ed.). Ballads, show tunes, other early 20th-century works by black songwriters include "Some of These Days," "A Good Man Is Hard to Find," "I'm Just Wild About Harry," "Love Will Find a Way," 31 other classics. Reprinted from rare sheet music, original covers. 160pp. 9 x 12. (Available in U.S. only)   40416-1

Available from your music dealer or write for ***free*** *Music Catalog to*
Dover Publications, Inc., Dept. MUBI, 31 East 2nd Street, Mineola, NY 11501
Visit us online at **www.doverpublications.com**

Dover Chamber Music Scores

Bach, Johann Sebastian, COMPLETE SUITES FOR UNACCOMPANIED CELLO AND SONATAS FOR VIOLA DA GAMBA. Bach-Gesellschaft edition of the six cello suites (BWV 1007–1012) and three sonatas (BWV 1027–1029), commonly played today on the cello. 112pp. 9⅜ x 12¼. 25641-3

Bach, Johann Sebastian, WORKS FOR VIOLIN. Complete Sonatas and Partitas for Unaccompanied Violin; Six Sonatas for Violin and Clavier. Bach-Gesellschaft edition. 158pp. 9⅜ x 12¼. 23683-8

Beethoven, Ludwig van. COMPLETE SONATAS AND VARIATIONS FOR CELLO AND PIANO. All five sonatas and three sets of variations. Breitkopf & Härtel edition. 176pp. 9⅜ x 12¼. 26441-6

Beethoven, Ludwig van. COMPLETE STRING QUARTETS, Breitkopf & Härtel edition. Six quartets of Opus 18; three quartets of Opus 59; Opera 74, 95, 127, 130, 131, 132, 135 and Grosse Fuge. Study score. 434pp. 9⅜ x 12¼. 22361-2

Beethoven, Ludwig van. COMPLETE VIOLIN SONATAS. All ten sonatas including the "Kreutzer" and "Spring" sonatas in the definitive Breitkopf & Härtel edition. 256pp. 9 x 12. 26277-4

Beethoven, Ludwig van. SIX GREAT PIANO TRIOS IN FULL SCORE. Definitive Breitkopf & Härtel edition of Beethoven's Piano Trios Nos. 1–6 including the "Ghost" and the "Archduke." 224pp. 9⅜ x 12¼. 25398-8

Brahms, Johannes, COMPLETE CHAMBER MUSIC FOR STRINGS AND CLARINET QUINTET. Vienna Gesellschaft der Musikfreunde edition of all quartets, quintets, and sextets without piano. Study edition. 262pp. 8⅜ x 11¼. 21914-3

Brahms, Johannes, COMPLETE PIANO TRIOS. All five piano trios in the definitive Breitkopf & Härtel edition. 288pp. 9 x 12. 25769-X

Brahms, Johannes, COMPLETE SONATAS FOR SOLO INSTRUMENT AND PIANO. All seven sonatas–three for violin, two for cello and two for clarinet (or viola)–reprinted from the authoritative Breitkopf & Härtel edition. 208pp. 9 x 12. 26091-7

Brahms, Johannes, QUINTET AND QUARTETS FOR PIANO AND STRINGS. Full scores of *Quintet in F Minor,* Op. 34; *Quartet in G Minor,* Op. 25; *Quartet in A Major,* Op. 26; *Quartet in C Minor,* Op. 60. Breitkopf & Härtel edition. 298pp. 9 x 12. 24900-X

Debussy, Claude and Ravel, Maurice, STRING QUARTETS BY DEBUSSY AND RAVEL/Claude Debussy: Quartet in G Minor, Op. 10/Maurice Ravel: Quartet in F Major. Authoritative one-volume edition of two influential masterpieces noted for individuality, delicate and subtle beauties. 112pp. 8¼ x 11. (Not available in France or Germany) 25231-0

Dvořák, Antonín, CHAMBER WORKS FOR PIANO AND STRINGS. Society editions of the F Minor and Dumky piano trios, D Major and E-flat Major piano quartets and A Major piano quintet. 352pp. 8⅜ x 11¼. (Not available in Europe or the United Kingdom) 25663-4

Dvořák, Antonín, FIVE LATE STRING QUARTETS. Treasury of Czech master's finest chamber works: Nos. 10, 11, 12, 13, 14. Reliable Simrock editions. 282pp. 8⅛ x 11. 25135-7

Franck, César, GREAT CHAMBER WORKS. Four great works: Violin Sonata in A Major, Piano Trio in F-sharp Minor, String Quartet in D Major and Piano Quintet in F Minor. From J. Hamelle, Paris and C. F. Peters, Leipzig editions. 248pp. 9⅜ x 12¼. 26546-3

Haydn, Joseph, ELEVEN LATE STRING QUARTETS. Complete reproductions of Op. 74, Nos. 1–3; Op. 76, Nos. 1–6; and Op. 77, Nos. 1 and 2. Definitive Eulenburg edition. Full-size study score. 320pp. 8⅜ x 11¼. 23753-2

Haydn, Joseph, STRING QUARTETS, OPP. 20 and 33, COMPLETE. Complete reproductions of the 12 masterful quartets (six each) of Opp. 20 and 33–in the reliable Eulenburg edition. 272pp. 8⅜ x 11¼. 24852-6

Haydn, Joseph, STRING QUARTETS, OPP. 42, 50 and 54. Complete reproductions of Op. 42 in D Minor; Op. 50, Nos. 1–6 ("Prussian Quartets") and Op. 54, Nos. 1–3. Reliable Eulenburg edition. 224pp. 8⅜ x 11¼. 24262-5

Haydn, Joseph, TWELVE STRING QUARTETS. 12 often-performed works: Op. 55, Nos. 1–3 (including *Razor*); Op. 64, Nos. 1–6; Op. 71, Nos. 1–3. Definitive Eulenburg edition. 288pp. 8⅜ x 11¼. 23933-0

Kreisler, Fritz, CAPRICE VIENNOIS AND OTHER FAVORITE PIECES FOR VIOLIN AND PIANO: With Separate Violin Part, *Liebesfreud, Liebesleid, Schön Rosmarin, Sicilienne and Rigaudon,* more. 64pp. plus slip-in violin part. 9 x 12. (Available in U.S. only) 28489-1

Mendelssohn, Felix, COMPLETE CHAMBER MUSIC FOR STRINGS. All of Mendelssohn's chamber music: Octet, Two Quintets, Six Quartets, and Four Pieces for String Quartet. (Nothing with piano is included.) Complete works edition (1874–7). Study score. 283pp. 9⅜ x 12¼. 23679-X

Mozart, Wolfgang Amadeus, COMPLETE STRING QUARTETS. Breitkopf & Härtel edition. All 23 string quartets plus alternate slow movement to K.156. Study score. 277pp. 9⅜ x 12¼. 22372-8

Mozart, Wolfgang Amadeus, COMPLETE STRING QUINTETS, Wolfgang Amadeus Mozart. All the standard-instrumentation string quintets, plus String Quintet in C Minor, K.406; Quintet with Horn or Second Cello, K.407; and Clarinet Quintet, K.581. Breitkopf & Härtel edition. Study score. 181pp. 9⅜ x 12¼. 23603-X

Schoenberg, Arnold, CHAMBER SYMPHONY NO. 1 FOR 15 SOLO INSTRUMENTS, OP. 9. One of Schoenberg's most pleasing and accessible works, this 1906 piece concentrates all the elements of a symphony into a single movement. 160 pp. 8⅜ x 11. (Available in U.S. only) 41900-2

Schubert, Franz, COMPLETE CHAMBER MUSIC FOR PIANOFORTE AND STRINGS. Breitkopf & Härtel edition. *Trout,* Quartet in F Major, and trios for piano, violin, cello. Study score. 192pp. 9 x 12. 21527-X

Schubert, Franz, COMPLETE CHAMBER MUSIC FOR STRINGS. Reproduced from famous Breitkopf & Härtel edition: Quintet in C Major (1828), 15 quartets and two trios for violin(s), viola, and violincello. Study score. 348pp. 9 x 12. 21463-X

Schumann, Clara (ed.), CHAMBER MUSIC OF ROBERT SCHUMANN, Superb collection of three trios, four quartets, and piano quintet. Breitkopf & Härtel edition. 288pp. 9⅜ x 12¼. 24101-7

Tchaikovsky, Peter Ilyitch, PIANO TRIO IN A MINOR, OP. 50. Charming homage to pianist Nicholas Rubinstein. Distinctively Russian in character, with overtones of regional folk music and dance. Authoritative edition. 120pp. 8⅛ x 11. 42136-8

Tchaikovsky, Peter Ilyitch and Borodin, Alexander, COMPLETE STRING QUARTETS. Tchaikovsky's Quartets Nos. 1–3 and Borodin's Quartets Nos. 1 and 2, reproduced from authoritative editions. 240pp. 8⅜ x 11¼. 28333-X

*Available from your music dealer or write for **free** Music Catalog to*
Dover Publications, Inc., Dept. MUBI, 31 East 2nd Street, Mineola, NY 11501
*Visit us online at **www.doverpublications.com***